D1568275

JOHN SCALZI

The
DISPATCHER:
Murder by Other Means

The DISPATCHER:

Murder by Other Means

JOHN SCALZI

SUBTERRANEAN PRESS 2021

First Print Edition

ISBN
978-1-64524-017-4

Subterranean Press
PO Box 190106
Burton, MI 48519

subterraneanpress.com

Manufactured in the United States of America

*For Dorothy Milne, the first person
to show me Chicago.
And Steve Feldberg, who gives me
an excuse to write about it.*

"**Mister Valdez, Mister** Peng here will pay you ten thousand dollars, in cash, to shoot him in the head right now."

The thing about this moment wasn't that someone was offering me a large sum of money to pick up a gun and put a hole in their skull with it. The thing about this moment was that this was not the first time in one month I'd been asked to do it.

But it was the first time I'd been asked to do it in the office of a major Chicago law firm, so I had that going for me, which was nice.

The Mr. Peng in question, with a young translator hovering directly behind him, stood by the desk of Lloyd Barnes, senior partner of Wilson Barnes Jimenez and Park. Wilson Barnes's offices took up three floors at

875 North Michigan, which most people referred to as the John Hancock Center for the same reason that the other very tall Chicago building was the Sears Tower, no matter who had the naming rights. Barnes himself sat at his very large, very modern desk, on which rested a number of intriguing objets d'art, a framed photo of his kids, and a Smith & Wesson M&P handgun, basic police issue.

I looked around the office and then turned to Barnes. He was the one who had summoned me with a promise of a job, shook my hand as I entered his office, and exchanged pleasantries and introductions before stating the nature of the business at hand. It seemed fair to address him first. "Your office has a lovely view of the lake, Mister Barnes," I said. "It would be a shame to ruin it with blood spatter."

"If everything goes well, it will only be blood-spattered for a few moments."

"It might not go well," I said.

Barnes smiled at this. "It's a risk I'm willing for you to take."

"You might be willing to," I replied. "I'm not sure I am."

"But this is your *job*," Barnes said.

I sighed and looked over to Peng, still standing there quietly while his translator murmured into his ear. "Is there a reason you want me to shoot and kill you, sir?" I asked.

Peng looked uncomfortable after this was translated for him. "I don't want to die. I just want to be shot," his translator interpreted after a moment.

I pointed to the Smith & Wesson. "That's not a surgical instrument. It's a weapon. This thing will blow out the back of your head, and no matter what else happens, you *will* die, sir. It's not going to be simple or pleasant. So you should have a good reason for me to kill you. And I should be able to know what it is."

Peng looked over at Barnes after this was translated. Barnes nodded at him. "I need to get to Beijing," Peng said, through his translator.

"There are *planes*," I said. "You could be there in fourteen hours. Brains intact."

"That's not fast enough," Barnes said.

I turned back to him. "Then you can explain why. Or I'm leaving."

"Mister Peng is in competition for a very important business deal in mainland China, and he reached an understanding with a major American bank for its funding," Barnes said, motioning to Peng. "Unfortunately, a competitor had the same idea and reached a similar understanding with another bank here in Chicago. That competitor is on a plane that departed O'Hare"— and here Barnes checked his watch—"twenty minutes ago. There's not another flight to Beijing for several hours. The deal is literally first come, first served.

Mister Peng needs to get there first. There's no other option."

"'First come, first served' doesn't sound like an entirely legitimate way for a major business deal to come together," I said.

Barnes smiled again. "These are exciting times in a competitive business environment, Mister Valdez. May I call you Tony?"

"Let's stick to Mister Valdez for now."

"Fine. As I said, exciting times. And as Mister Peng's American law firm, we're committed to helping him achieve his success."

"You'll be paid no matter what happens, though," I said.

"Of course. But if he's successful, we'll be paid more," Barnes said.

Peng spoke again, noticeably curt. "Mister Peng wishes to know what the problem is," his translator said. "He expected to be done with this by now."

"The problem is that what you're asking me to do isn't actually legal," I said. "The problem is that if I help you, and something goes wrong, the person who is on the hook is me."

"We've thought of that," Barnes said.

"Have you."

"In the event things go wrong, I and Mister Chen here"—Barnes motioned to the translator—"will say that Mister Peng became despondent after failing to convince you to help him."

I caught the implication of what was carefully not being said. "Is Mister Peng aware of this?" I asked Chen.

"Yes," he said.

"Ask him to confirm that to me."

Chen asked the question. Peng responded. "He says that if you do not help him now, he's ruined anyway." Peng looked me directly in the eye as Chen said this, and then nodded at the end of it. I nodded back. We understood each other.

"Ten thousand dollars in cash, Mister Valdez," Barnes said, coming back to the matter at hand.

"Twenty-five thousand," I said.

Barnes looked a bit shocked. "Excuse me?"

"That's my fee. For the shooting and for the risk."

"I just told you we have a cover story for you."

"It's not good enough." I motioned to Peng. "This month I've had two other proposals just like this one, for similar amounts of money. This is apparently a hot new trend in travel. I don't really do jobs like this, Mister Barnes. So if these offers are finding me, then others in my field are also getting offers. If they're getting offers, then somewhere along the way, someone's probably gotten sloppy. And when that happens, the police aren't going to be far behind."

I addressed the translator. "Mister Chen, are you a citizen?"

"Pardon?" Chen asked.

"Are you a United States citizen?" I asked.

"I'm Chinese," he said. "I've been here since I was three. I have a green card."

I turned back to Barnes. "The minute Chicago PD sees Mister Chen here, they're going to get Immigration to lean on him, hard."

"I won't tell," Chen said.

"It's easy to say that *now,*" I said. "Let's see what you have to say when a detective tells you that you're an accomplice to first-degree murder, and that the best-case scenario is that you're deported to a country you don't know or remember."

Chen shrank back, silent.

"What happened with those other two offers?" Barnes asked.

"I turned them down. Just like I'm going to turn this one down. Unless you meet my price."

"Pay him," Peng said to Barnes.

"It's a lot," Barnes replied.

Peng said something to Chen, his English apparently exhausted. "We're arguing over a stupid amount of money," Chen said. "Ten thousand, twenty-five thousand, who cares. I need to get to Beijing now. We're wasting time."

Barnes looked over to me. "Well, then. You have your money, Mister Valdez."

"In cash."

"It's in the wall safe. We'll settle up afterward."

"Fine," I said. Then. "Just one more question."

"What is it?" Barnes asked.

"Why me? I've never done work for you before, Mister Barnes."

"You came recommended. A mutual friend. He said you'd say you didn't do things like this much, but that was because you'd been lying to yourself about the reasons why." Barnes leaned back in his chair and spread out his hands. "I'm not here to judge one way or the other. I'm just glad you're agreeable."

"The gun's going to make a lot of noise," I said.

"I already told my assistant we'd be firing a blank for evidentiary reasons. We won't be bothered," Barnes said.

"Unless something goes wrong."

"Let's worry about that if it happens."

I didn't have anything to say to that. I picked up the gun, checked to make sure it was ready to fire, and then looked around. The office was on a corner with two sides of window glass. One of the other walls was shared with another office. That wouldn't work. I pointed to an area on the fourth wall that jutted out from the rest of the wall and featured shelves, on which were books and awards. "What's on the other side of that wall?" I asked.

"I have a private bathroom," Barnes said.

"Follow me," I said to Peng, and entered the bathroom. He followed, Chen trailing behind.

"Why are we in here?" Peng asked, through Chen.

"Because it can be hosed down," I said.

Chen turned green and then translated, stuttering. "I can wait outside," he said when he finished. He looked like he was about to throw up.

"You probably should," I said. He nodded numbly and exited.

I'd killed dozens and possibly hundreds of people during my professional career, and each one presented its own set of challenges. The challenge here was to minimize damage and to make it look like it was Peng, not me, pulling the trigger. I thought about it and paced around the bathroom, figuring angles, opening shower doors, and moving things around. Peng watched me as I did this, with some curiosity. He was a cool customer, if nothing else.

When I figured out what I wanted, I positioned Peng, who cooperated. There was a bathrobe on the door, for when Barnes used the shower. I stripped off my shirt and put the robe on, and placed a hand towel over my firing hand. The idea was to minimize gunshot residue on me in case things went poorly. Peng watched everything but didn't comment. I could tell he was becoming impatient.

"How much English do you know?" I asked.

"A little," Peng said.

I raised the gun to his temple and placed my index finger, covered by the towel, on the trigger guard. "I'm going to count to three and shoot. Understand? One, two, three, bang."

"Yes." Peng nodded curtly.

"Good. One," I said and pulled the trigger.

And then Peng was dead, and I was momentarily deaf except for the monstrous ringing in my ears caused by a handgun going off in an enclosed space. In retrospect I should have remembered that was going to happen. This was not the first time I had killed someone in an enclosed space.

Peng's body slumped on the floor, lifeless, for several seconds.

And then it disappeared, leaving Peng's clothes behind.

Not just his body disappeared. Also the bone and brain matter that the bullet had blasted out of Peng's head, and the blood that had poured out of the wound. All of it, in an instant, gone like it had never been there at all, the only evidence of any violence being the spent bullet lodged in the wall of the shower stall. The bullet would be clean as well—any bits of body on it removed as if by magic.

This didn't always happen. Sometimes when the bodies popped, blood remained on the clothes. The speculation was that if the blood was from a non-fatal injury, it stayed behind.

Peng's injury was definitely fatal. There was nothing left behind.

This was only an anecdotal observation. It wasn't really possible to do an actual scientific study. When you killed people these days, nine hundred and ninety-nine times out of a thousand, they came back, reappearing at their homes, or wherever else they felt safe, naked, no matter where in the world they were killed. But that one time out of a thousand, they stayed dead. That put a damper on any willingness to do a study.

It was also why people like me had jobs. We were licensed, bonded, insured killers. We didn't call ourselves killers, of course. We called ourselves dispatchers. We helped those about to die a natural death by killing them first. We gave them a chance to come back and keep living. We'd been doing it for a dozen years now, ever since the first attempted murder ended up with the victim alive, at home, naked, and confused.

We saved people's lives by killing them.

And occasionally we did other things, too. Like shooting Chinese businessmen in the head so they could magically appear at home in Beijing and beat their competitors to a contract.

Which wasn't technically in the job description. People were supposed to be at or near the edge of natural death before we could "dispatch" them. Killing them when they were perfectly healthy was not a thing we were licensed to do. Killing them for the purposes of transportation was obviously out. If you were a dispatcher caught doing that and you were lucky, you would only lose your license. If you weren't lucky, and it was the one time out of a thousand a dead body was left, then you were looking at a first-degree murder charge.

Fortunately, that wasn't the case this time. The only thing I could be charged with at the moment was reckless discharge of a firearm. I wasn't going to be on the hook for that, of course. Barnes wouldn't bother. I had done him and his client a service. I was a specialist. Someone who could do a job he wouldn't do, that the translator Chen certainly wasn't going to do, and that Peng couldn't have done himself.

"I was wondering when you were coming out," Barnes said as I emerged from the bathroom, washed up and redressed in my shirt. I had left the pistol in the bathroom, on top of the bathrobe. "Peng just called from his home outside Beijing. He arrived safe and sound. He scared his cat."

"That's good news for everybody but the cat," I said.

"Yes, well." Barnes got up to open his wall safe and motioned toward his bathroom as he went. "What's the damage?"

"You're going to need a new shower stall."

"If that's the worst of it, I'm not going to complain." Barnes opened the safe and pulled out three packets of hundred-dollar bills, each worth ten thousand dollars. He returned to his desk, broke open a packet of hundreds and began to count out fifty of them. While he did this, Chen went into the bathroom. He returned with Peng's clothes and effects, which he had neatly folded, and placed them on Barnes's desk. I assumed they would be shipped.

Barnes reached into his desk to get two small binder clips for the packet he had broken up, and placed a clip on each of the new, evenly distributed piles. One pile he placed on top of the two unbroken packets, and then he handed the entire stack to me. "Twenty-five thousand for you." Then he took the remainder and tossed it at Chen, who caught it awkwardly. "And the rest for you. If anyone asks, these are consulting fees. It's in your interest that no one asks. I know I don't need to remind *you* of this"—he pointed at me, and then pointed at Chen— "but I need to be sure you understand me, Mister Chen."

"I understand you," Chen said.

"Good. Then you can go."

Chen stuffed his five thousand dollars nervously into his pocket and departed the office quickly enough that he almost tripped himself going through the door.

"Do you think he's going to be a problem?" Barnes asked me.

"There's nothing for him to be a problem about," I said.

"And how about you?"

"I'm thankful you and Mister Peng asked me to consult on an international initiative to share information between American and Chinese dispatchers. Whether anything ever comes of it from this point forward is an open question."

"Good," Barnes said. "And should I keep you on file for future consulting in this area?"

I was about to say *no,* and then glanced down at my twenty-five thousand dollars.

I had avoided going back to this sort of not-quite-legal work. But the fact was I had just solved a number of problems for myself by dispatching Peng. Legitimate gigs were harder to find these days; the ones I used to have dried up some time ago. And I had more problems on the way, most of them involving money.

"Sure," I said finally.

"Good." Barnes nodded at the cash in my hand. "Would you like an envelope for that?"

"Please."

Three minutes later I was in the elevator with Chen, who was compulsively patting the pocket his money was in. My own money, now in a plain manila envelope, was stuffed into the inside pocket of my jacket. I did not feel the need to touch it in any way.

"You should stop that," I said. "Tapping your money."

Chen immediately stopped. "I didn't know I was doing that."

"I know. It's why I pointed it out."

"What should I do with it? The money, I mean?"

"I'm going to put mine in the bank."

"But—"

"But nothing," I said. "It's a consulting fee. Perfectly normal, perfectly legal. There's no reason I shouldn't deposit it into the bank. At least I can't think of any. Can you?"

Chen thought about it a minute. "No," he said.

"Well, then."

"I've never done that before," Chen said after a few seconds. He clearly wanted to talk about what had just happened. I was sympathetic and also wished there were other people in the elevator, so he would have been too nervous to bring it up.

I turned to face him directly. "Mister Chen, may I give you some advice?"

"I, uh…sure."

"You're a translator. What's the most important part of your job?"

Chen looked confused. "Accurately translating what my client—"

I held up my hand. "Trust. Trust is the most important part of your job. If your client doesn't trust you, it doesn't matter how accurately you translate the words. If you can't be trusted, you won't get work. Trust means different things, depending on the circumstances. Let me suggest to you that at this moment, trust means keeping certain things confidential. And to yourself. No matter how much you want to or even think you *need* to talk about it. Do you understand what I'm saying?"

Chen nodded.

"Good," I said.

The doors of the elevator opened to the lobby. We got out and went to the street. I hailed a taxi.

"It's just that I was scared to death," Chen said to me as I was getting into the taxi.

"Sure," I said, and got in. "Just remember that these days, there are worse ways to be scared."

I closed the door and the taxi pulled away, leaving Chen on the curb.

CHAPTER TWO

I wasn't entirely truthful to Chen the translator. I wasn't going to deposit all of my twenty-five thousand dollars into my bank. In the United States, if you walked into a bank with more than ten thousand dollars in cash and attempted to deposit it, the bank had to fill out paperwork, which alerted the government to that transaction. Too many of those, and the IRS and the Treasury Department would get suspicious.

To be fair, my particular transaction was, in fact, suspicious. Not "major drug trafficking" suspicious or even "shady mid-level marketing" suspicious. But large enough, given my line of work, that if anyone at the IRS was paying attention, I might get red-flagged. I didn't need that in my life at the moment. What I was doing was small potatoes, in the general scheme of legally shaky endeavors. But the

IRS liked going after the small potatoes. The small potatoes put up less of a fight when you mashed them.

The good news, such as it was, was that early in my career as a dispatcher I had learned the financial tricks of the trade that would help me in a moment such as this. When presented with a large chunk of cash that the government might look at suspiciously, the first step was: Spend a lot of it.

My first stop was my building manager, who happily accepted three months' rent in advance. This wasn't the first time I'd paid in advance or in cash. She was always happy about both. We were both happy, since six hours before I had been wondering how I was going to pay this month's rent.

The second stop was the currency exchange store on Division, where I bought my usual set of money orders to pay this month's collection of bills. This time the bills included the quarterly estimated tax payment that I, alas, as a freelance worker, was obliged to pay. Yes, there was some irony in paying the IRS from the amount of money I was trying to spend down in order to keep the IRS from being too interested in my money. On the other hand, the IRS would be interested in me anyway, if I didn't pay them what they thought I should owe them. The IRS was a fickle beast.

The third stop was grocery shopping at the Jewel-Osco, restocking my pantry, which had been getting

THE DISPATCHER: Murder by Other Means

low. This was followed by a small shopping spree at local stores to get new clothes and household essentials. Nothing fancy, nothing that would call attention to itself, just things I needed and wanted.

I stopped by the dentist to pay for the fillings I'd been paying off in installments. I was happy that I no longer had to worry about having my molars repossessed.

Then a quick hit on the bookstore on Milwaukee. Not too many books. I was running out of space in the apartment. Only five. Okay, six.

By the end of it, I had drawn down my cash considerably and relieved most of the immediate financial pressures bearing down on me. But I still had a slightly suspicious amount of cash left. Half of that I put into my personal fireproof safe in my apartment. It kept my passport, birth certificate, and other important papers, as well as a GPS tracker in case anyone got it into their head to steal it. I usually kept some amount of ready cash in there for emergencies. There had been no cash in the safe. Now there was.

The second half of the remaining cash I took to the Cermak Savings Bank, the one on Damen, right by the El stop.

"Hello, Mister Valdez," said Clari Santos, as I stepped up to her teller window. It was a small bank branch, so there were only two tellers and one manager, Ted

Gross, whose office was crammed into the back. "Cash deposit again?"

"You know me so well," I said, passing over the cash and the deposit slip.

She glanced down at the amount I listed to make sure she wouldn't have to do any additional paperwork, and seemed pleased she wouldn't have to. She took my money, put it away, and then clacked at her computer for a moment. "You have this going into checking. Would you like to put some of it into your savings account?"

"I'd forgotten I had a savings account."

She glanced back down at her computer screen. "You have one. It's been...inactive for a while. We could start that up for you again. We have really good rates right now."

I was going to ask what exactly constituted good rates in this day and age, when I noticed her eyes track behind me and go very wide. I turned to see what she was looking at.

It was four men, in masks, entering the branch. They had guns and duffel bags in hand.

And I have to confess that in that very moment, my first thought was *thank God Clari took my money; now it's insured by the FDIC.*

My second thought was more on point. It was *oh, shit.*

My third thought on the matter, a second later, was to note that there were twice as many bank robbers as there were customers. I was the only one at a teller. An older woman stood at the bank's center island, back to the robbers, studiously filling in a deposit slip for a check. She was entirely unaware of what was going on.

At least until one of the robbers coughed, and she looked up and behind her. At which point she started screaming in what I thought might be Vietnamese.

This seemed to remind the robbers what they were there for. One went to the woman, forcing her down and holding his gun on her. Another came toward me, telling me to get down and for Clari and the other teller to get their hands up. A third stationed himself by the door, acting as lookout. The final robber marched into the back, to Ted Gross's office. From my vantage point on the ground I couldn't see either the robber or Ted, but I heard a shocked yell, followed by the sound of his office door slamming shut.

In the space of ten seconds, everything was quiet again except for the sound of the old woman sobbing.

"Dude," the robber holding the gun on the woman said, to the one holding the gun on me. "What the fuck are you waiting for?"

The robber with his gun on me stood blankly for a moment, then trained his gun on Clari and threw his duffel bag at her. "Fill it," he said, and then he motioned to the other teller with his gun. "And then give it to your friend and have him fill it, too." His voice was cracking and stressed.

While his attention was elsewhere, I had a decision to make.

A dozen years ago, the calculus in situations like this changed. Before, criminals with guns held the certain threat of death. Disobey them and they would kill you with a shot through the head or chest. You were dead forever. This was, as it always had been, a keen motivator not to risk one's life.

Now, however, that rule didn't apply anymore. If a robber killed you, you almost never stayed dead—you almost always came back, naked but safe in your own home. With that, the threat of death wasn't much of a threat at all. In fact, depending on the circumstances, getting yourself killed might be the safest way of getting yourself out of harm's way.

When people began to realize that, acts like robbing banks became more risky—for the robbers. People were less afraid of rushing the robbers and disrupting the flow of the robbery. There was even a certain segment of the population—not a very smart segment—who looked forward to opportunities to be heroes and to bring down robbers, muggers, and other criminals who previously had the promise of deadly force on their side.

Most of these people, it had to be said, forgot that in most cases when people were shot, they weren't killed.

The bullets just did awful but non-life-threatening damage, leaving the victims with temporary and sometimes permanent disabilities, and huge medical bills. People who craved being a hero never thought about what it might be like to live without a leg or a pancreas.

For all that, at this moment, it was possible and even likely that from my crouch on the ground, I could tackle this robber by the legs and bring him down. If I did that, the calculus of the robbery would change.

The question I had to answer quickly was whether that calculus would change for the better for me and for the others who were being robbed. Whether I would be helping the situation, or just adding confusion and chaos and making things worse. I had no interest in being a hero for its own sake. I, more than others, knew about the real-world potential cost of such an action.

Also, there was the fact that I, like anyone, could still die. There was always that one time out of a thousand.

My robber seemed to figure out what I might be thinking, because he brought his gun back on me. "Stay down, Tony," he said. "I won't kill you. But if you move, I *will* hurt you."

Any response I had to that was taken away by the sound of a gunshot from inside Ted Gross's office. Both tellers and the old woman screamed. The robbers jumped. And in the silence that immediately followed, there were distant sirens, getting closer.

I heard a door opening, and then the fourth robber was back into my view.

"You did it?" the robber by the door asked.

"Yeah, I did it," the fourth robber replied.

"Then let's go," the robber by the door said.

The fourth robber nodded and then looked over to the second teller, who stood frozen, duffel bag in one hand, cash in the other. The robber grabbed the duffel bag from him, looked inside, then zipped it up. "Get down," he said. "All the way down. On the floor." I saw Clari and the other teller disappear from view.

As they did, all the robbers converged on me. I stayed down. The fourth robber looked at me and pointed his gun. "All the way down," he said. "Sprawl." I sprawled on the floor. As I did so, I could see out the window the first of the Chicago Police units arriving.

So did the robbers. "They're here," the one who had been watching the door said.

"Are you all ready?" the fourth robber asked. The other three robbers agreed that they were.

And then the fourth robber shot them all in the head. One, two, three.

In the same order—one, two, three—they fell.

Then they disappeared. One, two.

But not three.

Three stayed on the floor, leaking blood and brain matter.

The fourth robber stared at the corpse for a moment as more CPD units arrived outside, and police officers started spilling out of their cars. Then he shot the third robber again. And again. And one more time.

Three stayed on the floor. He was dead. And he wasn't coming back.

"Fuck!" yelled the fourth robber.

Then he charged the bank door, running toward the police. He kicked the door open, squarely planted himself, raised his gun and fired a shot, and then jerked like the proverbial marionette as roughly a dozen police bullets entered his body.

It disappeared before it even reached the ground.

Seconds later the police were through the door of the bank, swarming the branch. Shortly after that one of them was standing over the body of the third robber.

"He's dead," I said.

"You sure?" she asked.

"He was shot in the head, in the neck, and twice in the chest. I'm sure."

"What about you?"

"I'm fine," I said. "Can I get up?"

She nodded. I sat up and got a good look at the dead robber. As good a look as I could get through the ruined mask, that is.

"Who shot him?" the cop asked.

I pointed to the now-shattered door, and the pile of clothes and duffel bag just beyond it on the sidewalk. "It was him."

"Why would he do that?"

"I think it was their getaway plan," I said.

The cop looked over at the duffel bag and then at the corpse of the third robber. "I don't think they thought out their getaway plan very well."

"I guess they didn't." I motioned to the corpse. "Any chance you can take that mask off him?"

The cop recoiled at that. "We need to wait for the detectives to get here. Why'd you ask?"

I pointed again. "Because this one knew my name. Whoever he is, I knew him. Or at least, he knew me."

THREE

The next day, a young detective named Greg Bradley dropped a photo onto my kitchen table. It was of a man, smiling and hugging a kid, presumably his own. "His name was Doyle Hill."

I picked up the photo. "Right. Doyle."

"So you *did* know him," prompted Bradley.

"He was a dispatcher. It's a small community. There's a couple hundred in Illinois. We have an online group. We keep in touch."

"Did you know him well?" asked the other detective in the room, from behind me, by the fridge.

I turned to look at her. It was Nona Langdon, who, as it happened, *was* someone I knew well.

"Define 'well,'" I said. I set Doyle's picture back down on the table.

"'Well' in this case meaning you would get text messages from him, asking if you were looking for work," Bradley said.

I saw where this was going. "Ah, you got a warrant for his phone."

"We did," Bradley said. He approached the table and tapped the photo. "And we know that a couple of days ago he sent you a text asking you if you were interested in a gig."

"If you know that, then you also know that I sent him a text an hour later saying no."

"We do know that," Bradley agreed. "We also know that between those two texts, you made a voice call to him, lasting nearly five minutes."

"Yes, that was me asking about the gig."

"The bank robbery," suggested Bradley.

I turned back to Langdon and pointed at Bradley. "He's new, isn't he?"

"First month in the job," she said.

"Okay." I turned back to Bradley. "It wasn't about any robbery. It was about a choke club."

Bradley looked over to Langdon and then back to me. "What the hell is that?"

"Have you heard of erotic asphyxiation, Detective Bradley?"

"Sure. It's when you strangle someone until they come."

"Not exactly right, but somewhere in ballpark," I said. "As you might imagine, with that sort of activity, there's a higher than usual chance of severe injury or death. Some people who practice it will tell you it's possible to do it entirely safely. Those are the people you never do it with. But there are others who believe they can do it more safely, in a controlled environment. So they get together at a set time to follow their enthusiasm. That's a choke club."

"So they have dispatchers show up to deal with…'accidents,'" Bradley said.

"You got it."

Bradley blinked at this, considering. "That doesn't make sense," he said eventually. "If they're already choking the crap out of their partner, what do they need someone like you for?"

"Because, Detective Bradley, there's an immense psychological distance between choking someone for erotic fun, and dealing with the fact that you've just strangled someone into possible fatal brain damage. Most people aren't equipped to deal with what happens after that point. A dispatcher is. Also, there are the people who are attempting autoerotic asphyxiation. You don't come back from that."

Bradley made a face at this, as I expected he might.

"Why was Doyle Hill asking you about this job?" Langdon asked.

JOHN SCALZI

"Because there aren't a lot of dispatchers who want to work a job that involves watching naked people strangling each other while they screw, or hanging themselves with a belt from a closet rod while they masturbate." I tapped the photo. "I guess Doyle thought I might be one of them."

"Are you?" Bradley asked.

I turned back to him. "You have my text for the answer to that."

"Why did you call him about the gig instead of just texting him?"

"I think you can guess the answer to that, Detective Bradley," I said. "Because sometimes the gigs I get offered aren't exactly legal."

"Like killing off people who are being strangled to death during sex."

"Actually *that* would be perfectly legal. Erotic asphyxiation is stupid, but if it's consensual it's not illegal. If things go badly, then the victim is in grave mortal danger, and a dispatcher is empowered by the state to act. The worst thing about it, as long as the dispatch is successful, is that the dispatcher has to file paperwork about the incident, which is recoverable with a Freedom of Information Act query."

"So don't go to a choke party if you're running for office," Langdon said.

"I would have stopped that sentence at 'Don't go to a choke party,' but yes," I agreed.

"You have something to back up this whole 'choke party' explanation?" Bradley asked.

"I wasn't there, so I can't say if it actually happened," I said. "But I can give you the name of the person who Doyle said was hosting it." I gave him the name; he wrote it down in his little detective's notebook.

"I don't get it," Bradley said, when he finished writing and closed his notebook. "Why take these jobs at all? Why bother?"

I motioned to Langdon. "She knows why."

"For the same reason cop salaries have been frozen the last two years," she said.

"And teacher salaries and sanitation salaries," I said. "Austerity budgeting will get you. For dispatchers, it means that fewer of us are stationed at hospitals, which are the stable gigs in our line of work. When the new budget was passed, I was already an on-call dispatcher, not one with a full-time position. I used to have a side gig consulting with the police"—I looked at Langdon when I said that; she looked back impassively—"but that sort of fell through, too. So I work a lot of side jobs."

"There's always bartending," Bradley said.

I laughed. "That's for cops and firemen. You guys get bartending and bouncing. We get choke parties."

"And robbing banks."

"Detective Bradley, if I had anything to do with that bank robbery, or knew anything about it, do you really think I'd be talking to you without my lawyer?"

"You have a lawyer?"

"I know a few. Most of them would already be yelling at me for talking to either of you without one of them present. So for now, Detective Bradley, I'm done talking to you." I pointed to Langdon. "You, I might talk to some more."

Bradley glanced at Langdon, who motioned with her head toward my front door. "There's a coffee shop a block over," she said. "Why don't you go get us some coffee? I'll see you there in a bit."

Detective Bradley looked like he was going to protest. Then he left, closing the door behind him a little more loudly than he had to.

"He seems nice," I said.

"He's fine," Langdon said. "He's still under the impression he has to prove himself to the rest of us."

"Does he?"

"Not really. As long as he's not on the take, we don't actually give a shit one way or the other." She motioned to me. "But it does mean he's not going to just swallow your alibi. Which, by the way, isn't much of an alibi at all."

"I can account for my whereabouts all day long before I was at the bank," I said.

"Fine," Langdon said. "Where were you?"

"I did a little consulting work for a law firm in the morning, then I paid bills and went shopping."

"Consulting work," Langdon ventured.

"It's why I was in the bank in the first place. I was depositing my fee."

"Paid in cash?"

"There's nothing wrong with cash," I said. "It spends easily."

"What about the rest of the week?"

"You've already subpoenaed Doyle's phone records," I said. "I can show you the GPS data on mine for the last month. It's not going to intersect with Doyle's at all. Outside of those texts and the phone call, we didn't have any contact with each other."

"Bradley would say that there are other ways of being in contact."

"I'm sure he would. But that doesn't mean I was. You know me, Langdon. Knocking off banks isn't my style."

"There was a lot you didn't tell me when you were consulting for us, Tony," Langdon said. "There's a lot about your style I didn't know about. Or know about now."

"I don't do robberies. Or choke parties," I said. "That's a start, anyway."

Langdon decided to change the subject. "There's something I don't get about the robbery."

"What is it?"

"Four men go into a bank, take money from the tellers and the manager, and then their big escape plan is to shoot each other in the head."

"It makes sense because you can't chase them that way. In theory, they disappear after they've been killed, and you have no way of knowing where they've gone. It's a great plan, as long as no one stays dead."

Langdon shook her head. "It's a great plan up to a point," she said. "But physical objects don't disappear. Clothes. Wallets. Duffel bags."

"Sort of," I said. "Foreign objects embedded into the body will go with the body. If you've got a pacemaker and you're killed, you'll come back with the pacemaker. Same with a titanium hip or dental work."

"How does that work?"

I shrugged. "How does any of this work? We know that's how it works because that's how we've seen it work. Just like we know that if you shoot someone in the head, all the blood and mess usually goes with them when they go. Did you get any DNA from the clothes of the other robbers?"

Langdon frowned. "No."

"There you go."

"But that's where I'm going with this," Langdon continued. "The robbers knew what they were doing. They knew how to escape and not leave evidence behind. But that leaves behind the final robber."

"And Doyle," I pointed out.

"But he was an accident. He was unintended. If everything had gone to plan, he would've disappeared along with the other robbers. We watched the security video. The last robber takes the duffel bag, shoots the other robbers, and then rushes outside, gun blazing, where he's shot up like swiss cheese by us."

"Suicide by cop."

"Which makes me ask what the point was at all," Langdon said. "There was no way he was getting out of there with the money. The money wasn't *embedded* into his body. So what was he really doing?"

"You know there's the old saying that smart people don't rob banks with guns," I said.

"I've never heard that saying."

"It's an actual saying."

"I'm not saying it's wrong. I'm just saying I've never heard it before. You said it was an old saying."

"It *is* an old saying."

"It's an old saying among three people, maybe."

"My point is," I said, pressing on, "maybe these robbers didn't actually know what they were doing, and when it all went wrong, they panicked. Especially the last one, who was stuck with the money and no escape."

"Maybe," Langdon said. "Or maybe they were smarter than we thought. Or you think, anyway."

"Why are you telling me this?"

"I'm not so much telling you as trying to make sense of it all." Langdon motioned to the door, out of which Bradley had disappeared. "Bradley and I talked to everyone at the bank earlier today."

"Everyone okay?"

"Freaked out but okay," Langdon said. "The branch manager was actually murdered, you know. That last robber put a gun to his head. But he plans to show up to work tomorrow, when they open his branch back up. Said he needed to get back on the horse."

"That's admirable," I said. "Stupid, but admirable. By law, you're supposed to be able to take time off for that. To recover and get counseling."

"I mentioned that to him. He said the best counseling he could have was getting back to work."

"That's not actually correct."

"I know, but I'm not his therapist. We asked him about the robbery and he gave us answers, but they weren't actually helpful. He's still messed up, and I think maybe he was intimidated by us as cops."

"Okay, so?"

"So, you know him. He's the manager of the branch you bank at."

I narrowed my gaze at Langdon. "Yes, and—?"

"So maybe you can go in sometime and talk to him."

"Why would I do that?"

"Because I'm not one hundred percent convinced these robbers were stupid. Because I have a hunch about something. Because I would appreciate it."

"I see," I said. "A little freelance consulting for you."

"Yes," Langdon said.

"Unpaid."

"Chicago is on an austerity budget," Langdon agreed.

I pointed toward the door. "And while your partner the boy scout is still actively considering me as a suspect."

"He's not my partner, we're just working the case together."

"That's kind of the definition of partner."

"It's not actually," Langdon said. "And anyway, he may suspect you, but I don't."

"Really. After all that crap about not knowing about my style."

"It's not about style."

"Then what is it about?"

"You didn't kill the last robber," Langdon said.

I blinked. "What?"

"You didn't kill the last robber. If you were in on it, when the last robber was trapped, I think you would've wrestled the gun away from him and shot him. Then he's dead and gone, you look like a hero, and there's nothing in your recent history to say that you were anything but in the wrong place at the wrong time. But you didn't do that. You just stayed on the ground like a coward."

"I'm not comfortable with the 'coward' part of this."

"I am. As a police detective, I want you to be a coward. Heroes make crime scenes messier. The thing is, you acted like a rational, scared person would. You stayed on the ground. You didn't have anything to do with it. Bradley will figure that out eventually. I don't see any reason to wait."

"I thought about tackling one of the robbers, you know," I said after a minute.

"I bet you did," Langdon replied. "I'm glad you didn't. Because then I wouldn't be able to trust you. But I do trust you. And now I need you to help me. Please."

CHAPTER

FOUR

"Mister Valdez, good to see you again," Ted Gross said, popping his head out of his door. He motioned toward his office. "Come in, come in."

I went in and looked around. The office was tiny, in keeping with the small nature of the branch, and barely had enough room for Gross's desk, with his computer, a small file cabinet, two chairs for customers, and generic art on the wall. The only indication that the office had been the scene of horrific violence two days before was the smell of outgassing from the brand-new industrial carpet on the floor—I assumed the previous industrial carpet would've had a bullet hole in it.

Gross motioned me to one of his chairs. "I understand you're thinking of putting some money into our CDs," he said. He sat at his desk.

"I am," I said, sitting. The chair creaked slightly in that way anonymous office seating did. "It seems like the right thing for me at the moment."

"CDs are a great investment," Gross said. "Safe, consistent, and federally insured." He paused his spiel. "Which reminds me. I want you to know that your deposit the other day was fully recovered and added to your account. You gave it to Clari before the event, and for our purposes that meant it was in our possession, even if it wasn't fully entered into our system yet. So even if something had happened to the physical currency you deposited, *your* money was secure."

"Thank you."

"You're welcome. Cermak Savings will be sending you an official letter confirming everything I just said to you, but I wanted you to hear it from me first."

"I appreciate that," I said.

"Of course, of course." Gross tapped his screen. "Now, do you know what kind of CD you're interested in?"

"There's more than one kind?"

"There's the standard CDs, which we offer for terms between six months and five years. There's our liquid CDs, which allow you to access your money without penalty, but come with a lower interest rate. We have zero-coupon CDs if you're willing to put your money out of circulation for a long time..." Gross stopped and looked at my face. "I went too far on terms, didn't I?"

"I understand you were speaking English to me," I said.

Gross smiled. "Let's start over. How much money were you thinking of putting into a CD?"

"Two, maybe three thousand." I was thinking Langdon had better appreciate me taking money out of my own control for her benefit, but I didn't say that out loud.

"With that amount I think you're probably best served with one of our standard CDs. How is your liquidity at the moment? I mean, how much of a margin do you have for bills and expenses right now?"

"I'm fine but I've been better," I admitted.

"Well, haven't we all." Gross typed into his computer and then swiveled his monitor over to me. The screen featured a list of CD types with interest rates. "Why don't we start with a six-month standard CD for you? It's a long enough term that you'll see some benefit out of it, but not so long that you'll put yourself into a tight spot, financially speaking. And if you're happy with it at the end of the term, we can just roll it over for another six-month term or longer, if you're up for it."

"Sounds good," I said.

"Good!" Gross smiled and got to work. He seemed in his element as he clacked on his computer, and a small part of my brain regretted that I was probably about to ruin his day with what I was going to ask him next.

"Was that your first time?" I asked.

"Was what my first time?"

"The other day."

Gross looked up at me, mildly startled.

"Being robbed," I said.

Gross looked relieved; I figured he'd thought I was going to ask about him being shot and killed. "Oh, no. No, no, no. Six years ago I was a loan officer in Joliet, and someone tried to rob us then." He frowned. "It wasn't much of a robbery, really. Some kid was high on something and walked in with his hand in a bag from the McDonald's across the street and told us it was a stickup. Then his fries started falling out of his bag and he lost his train of thought. He started eating the fries off the carpet, and then he sprawled out and fell asleep. He was snoring by the time the police arrived."

"Kind of a best-case scenario for a robbery," I said.

"It was," Gross agreed. "Not at all like the other day."

"The other day was a lot."

"Yes." Gross stopped pecking at his computer for a moment, as if trying to figure out something, and then started pecking again. "Yes, it was."

"You okay?" I prompted.

"What?" Gross shook his head. "I'm fine. Fine. Well, not *fine,* but you know what I mean, right?"

"I'm not sure," I admitted.

"I'm as fine as I think you can be after something like that. After a robbery like that. After..." he trailed off.

I didn't say anything, and I waited.

I wasn't a psychologist or a therapist. But I dealt in death on a regular basis. When people found out I was a dispatcher, they opened up. About death. About people they knew who had died or had been dispatched. About their own fears and beliefs about death. About what they thought happened after death.

I thought they opened up because they believed that as a dispatcher, I had a special relationship with death. That I knew something about it that they didn't know, especially now, in a world where against all logic, some people came back from the dead so reliably that a profession was created to facilitate the process. My profession.

The fact was, I didn't know any more than anyone else. No dispatcher did. We didn't know why, twelve years ago, the murdered no longer stayed dead. We didn't know why people who died natural deaths stayed dead even now. We couldn't say why what we did worked. Just that it did.

People wanted to talk to us anyway. Most of the time, it was kind of a pain in the ass. All the dispatchers I knew got tired of talking about death with family and friends, with strangers and on dates. By the time you'd been a dispatcher for a couple of years, you'd probably had every possible conversation there was to have on the subject of death. You'd probably have those same conversations, over and over again, for the rest of your natural life.

And because you'd had those conversations about death, over and over and over again, as a dispatcher you knew when those conversations were about to start. The look people got just before they began. How they'd lean in confidentially and uncomfortably, as if to ask something they knew was taboo but they just *had* to know. How they'd lower their voices to keep the discussion just between the two of you, even if you were on a desert island and there was no one else around for thousands of miles.

Ted Gross had that look.

About damn time, I thought. I was beginning to think he'd never get there.

Gross leaned in. "Can I ask you something?"

"Sure," I said.

"You're a dispatcher, right?"

"That's right."

"So you see death all the time. On the job."

"Not all the time, no. We mostly do what we do as insurance. So that if things go wrong, there's an opportunity for the person to come back."

"But you've *killed* people," Gross pressed.

"Yes, of course."

"Were you scared? The other day, here?"

"Of course I was."

"Even though you know people come back. Even though you've killed people."

THE DISPATCHER: Murder by Other Means

"One doesn't have much to do with the other," I said. "When I'm doing my job, it's usually in a controlled environment." I paused at this and thought back on dispatching Peng the other day. That was not exactly a controlled environment. But it wasn't worth it to confuse Ted Gross about it at this moment. I kept going. "The robbery wasn't a controlled environment. Too many things could have gone badly. And anyway, I wasn't on the job. I wasn't a dispatcher when the robbery went down. I was a bank customer."

"I'm sorry about that," Gross said.

"It wasn't your fault."

And here Gross paused and something passed over his face—a flicker or a shadow of something. I didn't let on that I had seen it. I'm pretty sure I wasn't meant to.

"Oh, I know it wasn't," Gross said, and smiled. "It wasn't anyone's fault."

"It was the robbers' fault," I suggested.

Gross laughed a little too loudly. "Good point."

"One of them paid for it, at least," I said.

Another flicker here, and this time it took. "That wasn't supposed to happen," Gross said, after a second.

"What do you mean?"

"I mean I don't think that was the plan." Gross tapped on his desk a bit. *"Their* plan. The robbers."

"I think their plan was to escape by shooting each other," I said. "I don't think their plan was that one of them was going to stay dead. I think that was probably really inconvenient for them."

"What do you mean?" Gross asked.

"If the dead robber had disappeared like the rest of them, all of them would've made a clean getaway. There was no physical evidence, except for their clothes and weapons, and I'm guessing they were smart enough to minimize any chance of fingerprints or other things like that. But the police have the dead robber—I think his name was Hill—and I imagine that right now they're going over his accounts and talking to anyone who knew him." I shrugged. "I mean, they talked to me about the robbery, and I was just a bystander."

"They talked to me too," Gross said.

"I'd imagine they would."

"Do you think that'll be the end of it?"

"Probably," I said. "Like you said, you didn't have anything to do with the robbery. Just like me. We were both in the wrong place at the wrong time."

"That's right," Gross agreed.

"Actually, in your case, you could probably sue Hill and the other robbers once they're found. Well, Hill's estate."

Gross blinked at this. "Sue them? For what?"

"Wrongful death," I said.

This got a hesitant smile from Gross. "I'm not dead, though."

"But you *were,* right?" I pointed at him. "I was here. I heard the gunshot and I saw the news later. If you'd been wounded instead of killed, you probably wouldn't be at work, you'd be in the hospital. Or at the very least you'd be wearing a bandage."

Gross looked down at his immaculate dress shirt and then gave me a hesitant smile. "I guess you're right about that."

"Right. So you were killed. Which means under the law you've got a classic wrongful death claim. That you came back isn't the point. The Illinois legislature specifically didn't change that law."

"How do you know this?" Gross asked.

"It was part of the curriculum for dispatcher licensing," I said. "It's because dispatchers are specifically exempted from wrongful death suits, as long as they're performing their duties under the law." I pointed to Gross's computer. "That way if a dispatch I do doesn't succeed, I don't have to try to cash out this CD you're setting up for me."

"Has this happened?"

"Have I been sued?"

"Have you had an...unsuccessful dispatch?"

"Not yet. But they do happen. Like the other day. Which was not technically a dispatch, but you know what I mean."

Gross paused again, trying to find the right way to proceed.

"I know what you're going to ask," I assured him. "Go ahead and ask it."

"Have you ever died?" The words came bursting out of him.

"Once."

"How?"

"I'd rather not say." I'd been thrown down an elevator shaft, which I didn't appreciate at the time.

Gross held up his hands, as if to acknowledge the boundary I put up. "Okay. But...how did you handle it?"

"Not well," I admitted. "It was scary to die and disorienting to come back. I threw up. Twice."

"So how did you get over it?" Gross asked.

"I didn't get over it. I just try not to think about it."

"I don't know what I was expecting. I never thought about what would be on the other side of it," Gross said.

"You never thought about what it would be like to be dead?" I asked.

"No, I did, I have," Gross said. "I mean, in that way you do in the middle of the night. Whether there's an afterlife, or a heaven or hell. My dad was Jewish and my mom was Catholic, so I got both sides of that growing up. I don't know what I was expecting. But I wasn't—"

"You weren't expecting nothing."

Gross pointed. "*Yeah.* That's it. I was dead and there was nothing. No heaven or hell or anything else. Just nothing. And then me on my bed. And then me thinking that the nothing state could've lasted forever. And that nothing's what's waiting for me the next time. And now I wish I didn't know that."

"Maybe it'll be different when it's for real," I said. This was a standard line of mine. Sometimes it worked.

It didn't work on Gross. "But that's just it. It *was* for real, wasn't it?" He pointed out to the main floor of the branch. "That could have been me instead of—you said his name was Hill?"

"Doyle Hill."

"It could have been me, not him. Me dead forever and not him."

I shook my head. "That's not the way it works. Every death is its own separate thing."

"Maybe. But I still feel like it could've been me. And it's not worth it. None of it is worth being dead. Nothing is." Gross looked down at his desk, and I spent several seconds pretending not to see him fight back his tears.

"Are you okay?" I said, when I thought enough time had passed.

"I'm fine," he said, looking up. "Sorry. It's been a rough couple of days."

"Maybe you should take some time off," I suggested.

"Yeah, I thought about it after it happened. And then I stayed up all night thinking about the nothing that I have waiting for me when all of this"—he waved his arms, as if to encompass all of existence—"is done. If

I took time off, that's all I would think about. So if it's all the same, Mister Valdez, what I'd really like to do is finish issuing you this six-month certificate of deposit. It's not a lot, but it's something. It's an actual thing. And that helps me, right about now."

FIVE

I left my apartment to meet Langdon and found Detective Greg Bradley loitering outside my building.

"Okay, I'll bite," I said as I walked down the steps. "What are you doing here?"

"I'm here to let you know the good news," Bradley said. "Your choke club story checked out. I went through Hill's texts and emails and found his client. The client remembers Hill mentioning you specifically as a possible 'safety officer.' That was the client's phrase, not mine."

"What an interesting euphemism," I said. I started walking. I was meeting Langdon at the local brewpub on North Avenue a couple of blocks over.

"It sure is," Bradley agreed, keeping pace. "You should know the client was upset with you. Because you passed on the gig, they had to cancel the club meeting for the month."

"I think that's probably for the best."

"You're not wrong."

"So this means I'm off your list of people to investigate," I said.

"Well, here's the thing about that." Bradley got out his little notebook and flipped through it to a particular page. "You didn't lie to us about not having any other contact with Hill, as far as we can tell, so that's good. But just because you told us about the choke club doesn't mean that you two didn't talk about other things."

"You're kidding," I said.

"Five minutes is a long time on the phone. Check it on your next call, you'll see what I mean. We're working through leads and a lot of them are in the dispatcher...I guess you would say 'community,' which you're part of, so we'll see if there are any other connections there."

"That seems tenuous."

"I know that word," Bradley said.

"I wasn't questioning your vocabulary skills, detective."

Bradley shrugged. "It's all tenuous, until it isn't. Sometimes the fishing expedition reels in a marlin, if you catch my drift."

"I doubt there are any marlins on this particular trip."

"I wouldn't expect you to say anything other than that. And you're not wrong. Just because you know people in common doesn't mean there's anything nefarious about it. You know Detective Langdon, for example. Worked with her, even. I don't assume she's involved in anything untoward, just because she knows you."

"Thanks," I said dryly.

"In fact, if you have any tips for dealing with her, I'd appreciate them," Bradley said.

"You two not getting along?"

"We have a professional relationship. Very, very professional."

"That sounds like Langdon."

"So she's always been like this."

"Langdon and I got along fine the times we worked together," I said. "We were friends, or at least friendly. I'm just not under the illusion that she wasn't using me for her own ends, or that she had an overly romantic vision of who I was."

"Did that bother you?"

"As long as the Chicago Police Department was paying my consulting fee, I was fine with it."

"And she's never leaned on you otherwise."

I stopped walking and turned to Bradley. "Am I supposed to pretend that you don't know I'm about to go see Langdon, detective?"

Bradley smiled. "I just want to make sure we're all working from the same set of facts, is all. And if there's something that you're going to share with Langdon, I'd be happy to know it, too."

"If I know anything, you'll know it when she does. If she trusts you enough to share it."

"That means you don't trust me," Bradley said.

"I don't know you."

"What do you want to know?" Bradley spread his arms. "I'm an open book, Valdez."

"What do you know about the other people involved in the robbery?" I asked.

"I can't tell you that."

I smirked and started walking again. "That's some open book, detective."

"I thought we were discussing me *personally,*" Bradley said, catching up. "I'm thirty-one. One kid. Divorced. Detective for a month now, you know that. Before that I was six years in the fifth and sixteenth districts. Good service record."

"Congratulations."

"My point is you don't *have* to work through Langdon, if there's something you want to share."

"Thanks," I said. "I'll keep that in mind." We turned the corner to North Avenue, and I started walking west.

"Do that," Bradley said. "And while you're keeping that in mind, I do have one bit of information that I want *you* to share with Langdon. In the interest of openness, and building trust, and all of that."

"What is it?"

"Well, as it happens, it's about you." Bradley brought his notebook up again. "Like I said, you were truthful to us, as far as I can tell. You didn't have any recent contact with Hill outside him asking you about that choke club gig. But here's an interesting coincidence, Valdez: You both visited the Hancock Center within twenty-four hours of each other."

"It's a big building, detective."

"Sure, and maybe he was just visiting the Cheesecake Factory. It's very popular. But Hill's got emails in his queue from Wilson Barnes Jimenez and Park."

"Okay, and?"

"And Langdon told me—in the spirit of openness— that the other day you did some consulting for a law firm. It's why you were at the bank, you were depositing your fee. The GPS data *you* provided—thank you for that, by the way—has you at Hancock that morning. Wilson Barnes Jimenez and Park is the only law firm currently in that building."

"It's a large law firm."

"It certainly is," Bradley said. "Would have to be to afford that place, especially these days. It's got two dozen listed areas of practice. It's even been in the news the last couple of days. You heard about that?"

I shook my head. "No."

"One of their international clients. Apparently about to be arrested for various white-collar crimes. He just up and disappeared. As I understand it, the FTC and SEC are very upset about it. China won't extradite him, if he somehow managed to get back there. That has nothing to do with any of this, of course."

"Probably not," I agreed.

"But interesting that you and Hill might visit the same firm, so closely together in time."

"It's a coincidence."

"I'm sure it is," Bradley said. "Coincidence. Tenuous. It's all tenuous until it isn't. You'll tell Langdon about it anyway, won't you? Because if she's leaning on you for information, Valdez, it's probably best she knows every little detail." He looked up at the awning of the brewpub we'd just arrived at. "This is your stop."

"You're not coming in?" I asked. "You can tell Langdon about your discoveries yourself."

"I have some other leads to follow up on. You can tell her. And let her know I asked you to tell her about them. I'll check with her later to make sure she got it." Bradley put away his notebook. "You two have a nice lunch. I'm sure you'll have things to discuss."

"Bradley's right, you know," Langdon said. We were waiting for our pizza. I was having a beer. Langdon, on duty, was having a Sprite. "It's a hell of a coincidence to have you and Hill at the same lawyer's and at the same bank robbery, all within a day of each other."

"You don't think he's on to something there, do you?" I asked.

"I don't think you and Hill have anything to do with each other, no. I also think the coincidence probably isn't a coincidence."

"I'm not following you."

"I'm not following me either," Langdon admitted. "It's a gut feeling. I don't have any evidence for it."

"Well, don't worry about that," I said. "Bradley's on it." I drank my beer.

Langdon watched me. "You're not worried about Bradley, are you?"

"I know cops tend to find what they want to believe," I said.

"That's not very nice."

"Tell me I'm wrong."

"Speaking as a cop, we don't find what we want to believe. But we don't think things are that complicated, because people aren't that complicated. The simplest explanation is usually the right one."

"Occam's razor," I said.

"Right." Langdon pointed at me. "You knew Doyle Hill. You were at the robbery. You were also at the same lawyer's office he was at a day before. Simplest explanation is you're connected in this somehow."

"That's great, except I'm not."

"Not that you know about."

"You'd think if I were connected to a bank robbery, I'd know about it."

"Maybe you're not that smart," Langdon said.

"Thanks." I drank again.

"My point is Bradley isn't wrong to be looking for a connection. He's not even wrong to suspect you. The last time I saw you, I said there were other ways for you and Doyle to have been in contact than just phone and text. A lawyer's office is one way."

"And I told you then that knocking off banks wasn't my style."

"I believe you," Langdon said. "And Bradley's right to continue to check you out. Unless you want to go into more detail about that 'consulting' gig you did at the law firm."

"I think that's covered under attorney-client privilege."

Langdon made a face. Before she could say anything, the pizza arrived—a massive, flat, squarish pie. She looked at it. "The hell?" she said, looking up at me.

"I told you it was a New Haven-style pizza."

"As a native Chicagoan, I protest."

"More for me."

I took a slice and started applying myself to it. After a minute Langdon took one of her own, and didn't appear to have any complaints from that point forward. We ate in silence for a few minutes.

"You went to see that bank manager," Langdon said, after she finished her slice.

"I did," I said. "I got a CD I didn't need, so I could have an excuse to talk to him. You're welcome."

"Thank you for prudently investing. What did you think about the manager?"

"He's involved."

"Did he say that to you?" Langdon asked.

"Of course not. Selling a financial product doesn't mean he confessed to participating in a crime. But when we talked there were signs."

"What kind of signs?" Langdon reached for another slice. I thought briefly of asking where her protest as a native Chicagoan had gone.

"He said that the robbery didn't go as planned, and later he said nothing was worth dying for," I said.

"That doesn't sound like much," Langdon said.

"It isn't," I agreed. "You had to be in the room. He talked like he knew what was meant to happen, and had agreed to it, but then it was different from what he expected. And of course it was. Someone died. Permanently."

"You didn't record this conversation."

"No. I didn't think about it."

"So basically you got nothing out of him."

"I didn't get any evidence. I got a gut feeling. You may've heard of them."

"Your gut feeling isn't going to help me convince a judge to subpoena his financials or his phone."

"What did you expect for free?"

Langdon pointed to the pizza. "I'm covering lunch," she said.

"Oh, well, in *that* case." I took another slice.

"Seriously, Tony, it's not much to go on."

"It's not," I said, after I swallowed. "But I think it's true anyway. You have your hunches based on being a cop and doing police work for years. I have my hunches based on being a dispatcher and listening to people talk about their experiences with death. People get confessional with me, Langdon. There's the things they tell me, and then there's the things they don't *know* they're telling me. You know what that's like."

"Sure," Langdon said.

"Ted Gross knew he was telling me how he felt about being murdered, and what he thought about death. What he didn't know he was telling me was that he'd been involved with the robbery, and nothing about it was what he expected. And that's what was throwing him for a loop, even more than the fact of dying and coming back." I pointed at Langdon. "And I think you already *knew* this, because you asked me to go talk to him."

"Yes," Langdon admitted. "I was hoping Gross might've been more confessional to you than he was, because you weren't a cop and his guard would be down."

"That might be a little much to ask of someone who participated in a felony."

"It was worth a shot."

"You wanted someone to confirm your suspicions," I said. "Here I am, confirming them. Ted Gross was in on the robbery."

"Now I have to figure out how."

"That's your job," I agreed. I ate some more of my second slice. "How's the rest of the investigation going?"

"It's going," Langdon said. "Bradley's doing a lot of the footwork and I'm working the judges to get sub-poenas. We're tracking Hill's steps for the last month through his phone and email, but he wasn't entirely stu-pid. There are gaps where his phone is off or it looks like he left it at home while he was out."

"How do you know that?"

"I pulled video from his closest El stop. There are times he's at the station and his phone's not."

"If a dispatcher has a gig we know is legally iffy, we'll leave our phones at home."

"That's sneaky."

I shrugged. "These are the tricks of the trade. As a dispatcher I'd tell you that leaving your phone at home isn't really all that unusual."

"Yet you had your phone on you when you visited that law office."

"And so did Hill," I pointed out. "Which pokes a tiny hole in Bradley's collusion theory."

"A very tiny hole," Langdon said. "And he's just got your word on it that this is a thing dispatchers do."

"I didn't expect it would dissuade him any."

"Do you want me to talk to him?"

I blinked. "You asking Bradley to lay off me isn't going to make him any less suspicious of me. If anything, it'll just make him more suspicious of you."

"I'm glad you realize that. I was checking to make sure you did."

"He doesn't think you like him much," I said.

"These days I don't like anyone much," Langdon said.

"I thought you liked me," I replied. "You bought me lunch."

"I'm even going to let you take this monstrosity home." Langdon pointed to the remaining pizza.

"You had two slices," I said. "Don't pretend that you didn't like it."

"I don't want to have this conversation anymore," Langdon said.

"Fine." I waved to our wait staff to get them to box up the remains, then turned back to Langdon. "Is there anything else you want me to do on this case?"

"No. Ted Gross was the only thing I thought you might have insight on. The rest I can handle. I can't afford you anyway."

"You got me for pizza," I said.

"And I know you're angling to get me to use you as a paid consultant again." Langdon made a small motion with her hands. "The department isn't letting us do that much anymore, you know that."

"I know. It's not a great time to be a cop or a dispatcher."

"It's not a great time," Langdon said. "Do you have any other marketable skills?"

"I became a dispatcher *because* I didn't have any other marketable skills," I said.

"I'm glad I'm letting you take the pizza home now." Langdon drank from her Sprite.

That was the end of my involvement in the case.

Until Detective Bradley turned up dead.

CHAPTER
SIX

"There's a panel van with two cops in it on my street," I said to Langdon, as she stood in my apartment building doorway. I had come down to meet her rather than just buzz her in. It had been three days since I last saw her. Bradley had died yesterday. The panel van arrived not long after.

"You weren't supposed to notice that," she said.

"They should've parked farther away."

"It's a short street."

"Also, they shouldn't actually be there at *all,*" I said.

Langdon sighed and pulled out her phone to text someone. Twenty seconds later the panel van pulled out from its parking spot and drove away, the driver looking at me and Langdon as she went by.

Langdon turned back to me. "Happy?"

"Not really. I want to know why it was there in the first place."

"It's complicated."

"I would hope so."

"Can I come in?"

"I don't know," I said. "Is my apartment bugged?"

"Apartment? No."

"I don't like the sound of *that.*"

"Look, let me in. We have to talk."

I let Langdon in.

"There's been a development in Bradley's death," she said. She stood in my kitchen; I took a seat at my table. "We took a look at his notebook. The last thing in it was that you were coming to see him last night, at seven. We think he died between eight and ten last night."

I narrowed my eyes at Langdon incredulously. "What are you saying?"

"I'm saying he mentioned in his notebook that you were planning to visit him, just before he died."

"I was here last night at seven," I said, motioning to the apartment.

Langdon nodded. "Your phone was. And you've also said to me that dispatchers sometimes leave their phones behind."

I glanced over at my phone on the table. Well, at the very least, now I knew they were tracking it. "Check the security camera in my apartment vestibule," I said.

Langdon motioned toward the hallway. "There's a rear exit."

"I had Chinese delivery at six. I'm on the camera in the downstairs hallway."

"Which is still enough time to get to Bradley's place. You're in Wicker Park. He's in Rogers Park."

"Then check *his* apartment's security camera."

Langdon shook her head. "He had a house. From when he and his wife were still together. No security cameras. And no shared walls for neighbors to notice any noise."

"Jesus."

"It would help if you had something other than your phone and food delivery to confirm you were here."

I spread my hands helplessly. "I was at this table, eating Chinese and reading a book. Alone."

"And you didn't have any plans to see or talk to Bradley."

"The last time I saw him or spoke to him was just before I saw and spoke to you," I said.

"No contact at all since then?"

"No. He was busy trying to link me to a botched bank robbery. I wasn't interested in helping him with that particular hobby."

"You understand his trying to link you to the robbery isn't a good thing for you," she said.

I waved in the direction of the street. "Since there were cops staking out my apartment, I'd guess not."

"Relax about the cops in the van."

"Why would I do that? Why would I relax about the cops treating me like a criminal?"

"*I* had the cops put there."

I was incredulous. "*You* really think I had something to do with Bradley's death?"

"No," Langdon said. "I think whoever did have something to do with it might come after you next."

That quieted me down.

Langdon pulled out a chair at the table and sat down. "Look, Tony. I told you it was complicated."

"Those cops were for my protection," I said.

"Yes."

"And that's the reason you gave for having them there on the street."

"No," Langdon admitted. "Every other cop in Chicago thinks you had something to do with Bradley's death."

"The Chicago Police Department thinks I'm a cop killer." I threw up my hands. "Well, that's just great."

Langdon shook her head. "That's not exactly it."

"Explain."

"Bradley's death was a suicide."

I paused at this. "That doesn't make any sense," I said.

Langdon peered at me intently. "Tell me why."

"All I know about Bradley is my time with him and what you told me of him. But none of that suggested someone who was suicidal. He loved his job, I know that much. I didn't like his enthusiasm for trying to link me to that robbery, but he was doing his job well. He wanted to find out what was going to happen next."

"That's right," Langdon said.

"No dark secrets in his past?" I asked.

"His service record was clean."

"He mentioned he was divorced and had a kid. Was that messy?"

Langdon shook her head. "Amicable. He told me they divorced because she realized she was gay."

"A lot of guys don't take that very well."

"He did. He said she was still his best friend. Their daughter lives with her but he was always out to Oak Park on the weekends, visiting."

"No depression or anything like that."

"Not that I knew of."

"No reason to kill himself."

"No," Langdon agreed. "And yet he did."

"But *you* don't think he did," I said. "And neither does the rest of the Chicago police force."

"No."

"You realize the problem with this."

"If he'd been murdered, he'd still be alive," Langdon said.

"Right. Whoever it was would kill him, and he would come right back."

"They killed him in his home," Langdon pointed out. "When he died, he'd come back in his house. Where they would be. And they'd try again until they got it right."

I shook my head. "That's not how it works."

"I'm pretty sure that *is* how it works."

"No, I mean, if they were doing that, they would probably still be at it," I said. "We say that people who get murdered only stay dead one time in a thousand. But that doesn't mean it's *cumulative*. You don't keep killing someone until they run out of chances to stay alive. Each time is a whole new roll of the dice."

"Whoever was killing him probably wouldn't know that," Langdon said.

"They might not," I conceded. "But that doesn't change the facts. And there's the other wrinkle."

Langdon frowned. "What other wrinkle?"

"Everyone says that when someone is murdered, they come back in their home, but that's not strictly true," I said. "Where they come back is to somewhere they felt *safe*. If Bradley's got people in his house who will murder him the instant he comes back, eventually he's not going to come back there. He'll come back at his parents' house. Or his ex-wife's house in Oak Park, because they're still friends and he loves his daughter."

"It could take dozens of attempts," Langdon said. Probably she was remembering the first case she and I had worked on together, a couple of years back. A husband was pushing experimental cancer therapies on his wife, and she was dispatched each time they failed. Finally, when she was dispatched, she didn't reappear at their home. She reappeared on their boat, which felt safer to her.

"It could," I said. "Or it might take a lot fewer, because in this case the theoretical people trying to kill Bradley were actually intending to murder him. That would be pretty unambiguous."

"You're saying that you don't doubt Bradley committed suicide," Langdon said.

"I'm saying what you already know," I said. "In this day and age it's almost impossible to murder someone and have it stick. If it looks like Bradley committed suicide, it's probably because he did."

"But you said yourself it doesn't make any sense."

"It doesn't make any sense," I agreed.

Langdon nodded and sat back. "And now you know why the Chicago Police Department wanted a couple of cops in a panel van watching you. And why I did, too."

"I'm not going to lie. I appreciate your line of reasoning more than theirs." I looked over to Langdon. "Are you going to be in trouble for coming here?"

Langdon smiled. "I was told to come. You trust me, Tony. So you would slip up in front of me."

"Did I?"

"You haven't given me a convincing alibi for your whereabouts before Bradley's death. You were the last person Bradley said he was planning to see before he died. You were being investigated by Bradley in connection with a crime. You know that's more than enough for us to stay interested in you."

"Despite the fact that the likelihood of Bradley's death being anything other than a suicide is incredibly low."

"Yes, despite that," Langdon said. "I don't believe it. No other cop who knew Bradley believes it. And you don't believe it, either."

"You'll be wasting your time," I said.

"Maybe."

"And what about you?" I asked.

"We're done," Langdon said. "For now."

"You don't believe I had anything to do with Bradley's death."

"Tony, right now it doesn't matter what I think."

"That's not the same thing."

"No, it's not," Langdon said. "Right now I'm not doing 'believe.' I'm working with what we have. And what we have right now is you, and Bradley's note. No cop who knew Bradley is going to let a suicide label stand. Not when they have an alternate theory of the case."

"The alternate theory being me."

"That's right." Langdon stood up. "I put those cops out there today because I wanted to protect you, Tony, long enough for me to talk to you myself. After this, their presence might protect you from whoever might come after you. But you know I can't protect you from *us*. You're on your own there."

"Any last suggestions?" I asked, looking up at Langdon.

"Yes," she said. "Stop talking to the cops. Including me. Get yourself a lawyer. And since I know you're about to be even less busy than you are now, because the Chicago Police Department will let your agency know you're currently under investigation in connection with a death, maybe you should find someone else for us to focus our attention on."

"Even if it was a suicide and no one else is to blame."

"It's like I said, Tony. No one believes that, even you."

"You said Bradley had my name in his notebook," I said as she turned to go. "Tell me you're looking at the other names in there, too."

Langdon turned back. "I can't tell you anything about that," she said. "I can tell you this. Bradley's notebook is spiral bound. When you tear out pages, little bits of the paper get stuck in the spiral. The pages are gone, but you can tell they were there at one point."

"Okay," I said. "And?"

"And there were pages torn out of his notebook. I don't know how many, and I don't know what was on them. The torn-out pages weren't in his trash, either by his desk or under his kitchen sink, and neither of them looked like they'd been taken out in the last couple of days. They're just gone. It would be interesting to know what was on those torn-out pages. Because at the moment, what's in the notebook points to you."

"If I was involved, why would I leave evidence that points to me?" I asked.

"That's an interesting question, Tony," Langdon said. "I hope you can come up with a better answer for it than the one we're going with at the moment."

"Which is?"

"That we don't know either, we're just glad you did. Also, Tony, you can do me one last favor."

"What's that?"

"The next pair of cops we put on you, pretend not to see. They're not going to take kindly to being spotted, and at this point, you don't want to piss any of us off."

SEVEN

I found Ted Gross at the cocktail lounge a block down
Damen from the Cermak Savings. It was the sort of place
that ostentatiously bans cell phones and has complicated drinks with names like "Text Me The Details" and
"Is This The Real Life." He was sitting at the bar, which
was tastefully low-lit, nursing something in a highball
glass. I knew he was in the lounge because I'd watched
him go there after his bank closed. I waited an appropriate time before going in myself.

The seat next to him was open; I took it. He didn't
look up. He was staring into his drink like he'd lost
something in it.

"What's that?" I asked, pointing to his drink.

This got him to look up. It took him a second to recognize me. "Valdez, right? Tony Valdez."

"That's right," I said. "You sold me a CD a few days ago."

Gross nodded and focused on his drink again. After a minute I thought he had forgotten about me, but then his brow furrowed. "I don't remember what this is called," he said. He looked over to the bartender, who was washing a glass. "What's this again?"

"That's the 'Come Back If It Starts To Swell,'" the bartender said. He was burly and had a full beard and a tattoo of Popeye on his arm. I wondered briefly if bartenders at this cocktail lounge were hired or cast.

"That's right," Gross said and turned back to me. "It's got egg whites in it."

"How is it?"

"It's the best drink I ever had that had egg whites in it," Gross declared. "What're you going to get?"

"I think I'm going to settle for an old-fashioned," I said, angling myself so the bartender heard the order, too.

"Put it on my tab," Gross said to the bartender.

"You don't have to do that," I said.

"I insist. You bought a CD. This is just basic customer service."

"Do you always buy your customers drinks?"

"I do when they're at the bar with me."

"If I'd known that was the deal, I'd have gotten a CD a lot sooner," I said.

Gross smiled and raised his glass. We sat quietly until the bartender brought over my old-fashioned.

"Cheers," I said.

"Cheers." Gross drank again, nearly emptying his drink with egg whites in it.

"Is this your usual after-work bar?" I asked.

"I've never been here before in my life," Gross said. "I always saw the sign when I came off the El in the morning, and I would think, 'I should check that place out.' But it's not open for lunch, and then when we close the bank I need to get home."

"But not today?"

"No." Gross did a little grimace and wobbled his head. "Well, yes. Eventually. But today I decided, fuck it, I'm going into that place. And now I'm here." He drained what was left in the glass and then tapped it on the bar to get the bartender's attention. "Another."

"Same thing?" the bartender asked.

"No," Gross said. "Pick something for me. Something you always wanted to make but no one ever orders."

"Okay, but it's going to cost more," the bartender said.

"Is it going to be worth it?" Gross asked.

"Hell yeah it is."

Gross made a sweeping motion with his hands. "Do it." The bartender grinned and got to it. Gross turned back to me. "And you? Is this your favorite bar?"

"I don't get in here much," I allowed. "It's a little more upscale than I can afford at the moment."

"Things are tough all over, right?"

"Something like that."

"But you're a dispatcher," Gross said. "People are always dying. Business should be booming."

I smiled. "That's not exactly the way it works."

"No. It never is." Gross waved to encompass the room. "But we're still here. The both of us."

"Yes, we are."

"Yes." Gross got a quizzical look on his face. "It's a little stupid to have visiting a cocktail lounge as a bucket list item, though."

"No one ever said your bucket list had to be all big things," I said. "They don't all have to be skydiving and visiting Paris."

"I never visited Paris," Gross said.

"I was there once."

"How was it?"

"Full of tourists," I said. "Including me."

The bartender brought over the new drink in a large cocktail glass. "Here you are, sir."

Gross peered at it. "Is there egg in this one?"

"Not this time."

Gross picked up the glass, swirled the contents gently, and took a sip. He smiled. The bartender smiled back. Gross set the glass down and fished out his wallet and slapped down a credit card and a $50 bill. "That's to settle the bill," he said, pointing to the credit card. He then pointed at the fifty. "And that's for you." The bartender nodded, took both, and went away.

"Hell of a tip," I said.

"Well, why not." Gross picked up his drink. "You only live once." He paused and looked over to me. "No offense."

"None taken."

"So if you don't come in here often, why did you come in today?" Gross asked, once he'd set his new drink down.

"If I'm being honest, I came in because you were in here."

Gross waggled a finger at me. "You know what, I *thought* that might be why. You want to talk more about the robbery."

"I do."

"You think I was involved with it."

I blinked. "What makes you think that?"

"Because that detective thinks I am. You got questioned by the police?"

"I was."

"Was one of them a black woman?"

"She was."

Gross nodded. "That's the one. She and another detective talked to me the day of the robbery and then she came back to the bank yesterday, alone. She had questions. Very specific questions. Questions about my relationship to Doyle Hill."

I almost asked *how do you know Doyle?* but then I remembered he didn't know I knew Doyle. Then Gross peered at me. "You knew Doyle, didn't you? You're a dispatcher, too."

I made a decision. "Yes," I said. "I knew Doyle."

Gross nodded. "I thought so. That's why you're here. You want to know what happened to Doyle, too." He drank from his cocktail glass.

"Did you tell the detective you knew him?" I asked.

"No," Gross said. "I told her that I wasn't going to speak to her anymore without a lawyer."

"Then why are you telling me?"

"You're not a cop. And because you knew Doyle. You were his friend." The bartender returned with the bill, the credit card, and a pen, and then went away again.

"How did *you* know Doyle?" I asked.

"We went to high school together," Gross said. "We were friends. Not, like, *best* friends. We knew people in common and went to the same parties. We were friendly."

"And you were still friends."

"We were Facebook friends?" Gross tilted his head to make sure I got it. "I saw his cat pictures, he saw the pictures of my kids, you know."

"Sure."

"I don't know, maybe the cops got a subpoena for my Facebook account and saw him post a cat picture or something. Anyway, now they know I knew him."

"Just because you knew Doyle doesn't mean you were in on the robbery," I said. "Maybe Doyle picked your branch because he already knew about it."

Gross smiled at me and tipped his glass slightly in my direction. "That's kind. You're kind. I like that you think that. But no. I was in on it." He drank again.

I waited until he was done taking his sip before asking the obvious question. "Why would you do that?"

"Because I needed the money, of course!" Gross said loudly. I looked around to see if anyone in the bar had turned their head to see why he was shouting, but no one had. "My wife doesn't trust the school system. She wants our kids in private schools. I make fifty-five thousand dollars a year, and she sells essential oils to her pals. Really *poorly*. We get the cash deposits of half the businesses in Wicker Park. All the ones that like working with a small community bank instead of, like, Bank of America." He motioned at the bar. *"This* place."

"So Doyle and his pals would come in, rob the place, take the cash, and then later on you'd get a cut."

"Right," Gross said. "Enough for a year of preschool and Montessori." He frowned. "But then it happened and things didn't go as planned."

"You mean Doyle not disappearing after he got shot."

"No. Well, yes, that too, but before that. When the other one came into my office."

"The other robber."

"Yes."

"You don't know who that was?"

"I only ever knew Doyle," Gross said. "The other one came into my office and told me to unlock my computer so he could access it. That wasn't part of the deal. Cash isn't a problem; whatever we have in cash is less than what people are insured for by the FDIC. But if this guy accessed member accounts, he could transfer people's entire savings or millions of dollars."

"And it would be on you because you let him in."

"Right!" Gross pointed at me for emphasis. "I tried to argue that and he punched me in the ear and told me if I didn't unlock my screen he wouldn't kill me but he'd make sure I'd be on a ventilator the rest of my life."

"Did you unlock it?"

"Of course I unlocked it. And as soon as I did, that asshole shot me dead."

"Which you never agreed to."

"Which I did *not* agree to!" Gross was yelling again. "I mean, are you kidding? Who agrees to something like that? Do people *ever* agree to that?"

This wasn't the right time for me to tell him that, in fact, others played the odds with death all the time, and their willingness to do so was what caused me to be at his bank when the robbery went down. Instead I shook my head *no*.

"Thank you," Gross said. He sipped again, finishing his drink.

"Did you tell the cops the robber accessed your computer?"

"No." Gross set his drink glass on the bar. "And for days I thought that I was going to get caught out. But nothing happened. No accounts were drained. No accounts at my branch were even accessed, as far as I could see. I got shot—got murdered—for nothing."

"That doesn't make any sense," I said.

"No." Gross picked up his empty glass, examined it, and set it back down. "No, it doesn't. None of it makes any sense." He looked up at me. "All I fucking wanted was to pay for my kids' schools, man. That's all I wanted."

"Mister Gross, you have to know the police are going to keep looking," I said. "Sooner or later, they're going to put the pieces together."

"They'll try," Gross agreed. "But I know something they don't know."

"What's that?"

Gross got up off his stool and motioned to me. "Come on. Walk me to the El station and I'll tell you."

I hesitated. "It'll only take a minute," Gross assured me. "I'm already late going home." He waved to the bartender and started walking out the door. I followed. We headed north, in the direction of the Damen El stop, a block and a half away. Gross pulled out his Ventra card and paid for me, and we walked up to the northbound platform together.

"Did you hear about the detective?" Gross asked me.

"The one you were talking about earlier? The woman?"

"No, the other one," Gross said. "The man. He's dead."

"How do you know?"

"The other detective—Langdon?—told me."

"Do you know what happened?" I asked. I already knew about Bradley, but Gross didn't know that.

"She said they considered it a suspicious death," Gross said. "But that doesn't really make any sense, does it? Hardly any deaths are that suspicious anymore."

"So you think something like a heart attack."

"Oh, no," Gross said. "A suicide for sure. Definitely a suicide."

"Why do you think that?" I asked.

Gross looked down the track for his train and then looked back and smiled. "Do you know why I'm talking to you, Mister Valdez?"

I smiled back. "I thought it was because I wasn't a cop."

"It's because you're in on it, too."

I stopped smiling. "Excuse me?"

Gross made a dismissive wave. "Don't worry, I don't expect you to admit it. But you're a dispatcher, like they were. You knew Doyle, too. It all fits together. I'm telling you because you already know. You already know all of this. Nothing I'm telling you surprises you at all. Does it?"

"No," I admitted. "Not really."

Gross smiled again. "Well, then. There's just one thing you don't know, and I wanted to tell you, because it's going to happen to you."

"What's that?"

"That they don't have to murder you to shut you up," Gross said. And then he walked off the platform, timing his fall onto the tracks to coincide with the arrival of the train.

EIGHT

"I thought we weren't talking to each other anymore," I said to Langdon as she walked up to me on the El platform.

"You don't leave me any choice," Langdon said. "You keep showing up in my case."

The platform was swarming with Chicago police taking statements from the people who were there when Gross walked himself in front of the train. An unhappy number of them had pointed at me while they were making statements. A small contingent of EMTs hovered. Gross was beyond their help, but someone would have to remove him from the tracks. Once they removed the train, that is, which remained parked at the station. A bunch of Chicagoans' evening commute had been irreparably delayed by Gross's final act.

I motioned to one of the cops taking statements. "I already told them I didn't have anything to say."

"I know. The thinking is you'll make an exception for me."

"You told me not to."

"I did," Langdon agreed, and waited.

"You already have the security video," I said eventually. "It shows him stepping out in front of the train."

"I'm sure it does. Did you try to stop him?"

"No. I wasn't expecting that he'd do that. By the time I realized it, he was already under the train."

Langdon's expression changed slightly. "Are you okay?"

"Not really," I said. "But I'll be okay. I'm used to death. Just"—I waved toward the stopped train—"not like this."

"Sorry."

"Thank you."

"Why did he do it?"

"I don't know."

"You were talking to him before he did it."

"Yes, but not about that."

"What about, then?"

"Banking."

Langdon gave me a look. "Banking."

"I bought a CD from him the other day, you'll recall."

"And that was intriguing enough that you followed him up here to the El platform."

"Apparently."

"Where did the conversation begin?"

I pointed in the direction of the bar, or where it would be, were it not obscured by a stopped train. "I was at a bar. Coincidentally he was there, too. We struck up a conversation."

"About what?"

"Kids. Commutes. Essential oils."

"Anyone to confirm this?"

"You might check with the bartender. Gross left a big tip. He'd remember."

"And this is the story you're going with, Tony?"

"Why wouldn't it be?" I asked. Langdon stared at me. I stared back.

"I'm not sure I like this version of you," she said after a minute.

"It's not my favorite, either," I said. "But here we are."

"Here we are," Langdon agreed. "Anytime you want to go back to a different version, let me know."

"I would, but we're not talking anymore."

Langdon sighed. "I deserve that, I suppose."

"Yes, you do."

"In that case, you didn't hear me say this." She motioned with her head past the platform, to the street below. "There's a guy loitering there. Tan windbreaker."

"I've seen him. You told me to pretend not to see him."

"I told you to pretend not to see *my* people," Langdon said. "He's not my people."

"Oh."

"Yes, 'oh,'" Langdon said.

"You can't arrest him?"

"For standing on the sidewalk? No. So do me a favor, Tony. Go home. Go home and stay there. They probably know I have your apartment watched. They're probably not going to try anything stupid there." Langdon walked away to confer with another cop about something or other. I watched her walk away, then turned to look at the stopped train again before heading down the stairs home.

Tan Windbreaker was standing in front of a doughnut shop, eating a doughnut because apparently tailing me was hungry work. I got out my phone, opened the camera app, and then put the phone up to my ear and started to talk like I was having conversation into it. As I walked by Tan Windbreaker, my finger clicked the down volume button, activating the camera shutter. I had muted the fake camera shutter sound months before, because fake camera shutter sounds are annoying. I got off several shots while appearing to order a pizza.

Then at the crosswalk, Tan Windbreaker behind me, I turned off the camera and actually did order a pizza. It had been a long day. I wasn't going to cook.

At home I opened the photo app on my phone and checked out the pictures of Tan Windbreaker. I had taken four photos, three of which were too blurry to be of any use, but one of which caught him in full color clarity. He looked late thirties, early forties, and had the sort of moustache that got associated with cops or low-level mob thugs. Langdon had said he wasn't one of hers, so maybe that sorted him into the "thug" category. I'd spotted him a couple of days earlier but hadn't worried about him too much, because I'd assumed he was a cop. To have him turn out to be something else was cause for concern.

But it doesn't actually mean he's a threat, my brain volunteered. *He could just be a dude who lives in the neighborhood. Wicker Park is bigger than you think.*

Which, okay. On the other hand, several people I was tangentially connected with had died in the last week or so, most under deeply suspicious circumstances, and this person, who I had never seen before in my life, was conspicuously out and about when I happened to be wandering by. He might not be a threat, but I didn't feel entirely ridiculous being a little paranoid.

I stared at Tan Windbreaker's picture again and frowned. Moustache aside, he was unremarkable. This probably came in handy for him if he was a low-level thug, but it didn't make identifying him easy. Just on the outside chance that it would be useful, I put his picture into Google image search. It turned up results for the doughnut shop behind him. He was so anonymous that even doughnuts were more conspicuous.

The intercom on the wall buzzed. My pizza had arrived.

"You're the large Hawaiian?" the delivery person asked me, and it took me a second to realize she was describing the pizza, not me.

"That's right." I handed over the tip; the pizza I'd paid for when I ordered it.

"I want you to know there was some discussion about whether to make the pizza."

"Because it's a Hawaiian pizza?"

"Yeah. We have a new employee who makes the pizzas. He considers pineapple on pizza against the laws of God and nature." She held out the pizza.

"And yet you have it on the menu," I said, taking it.

"He said that just because it's on the menu doesn't mean it should ever be ordered," the delivery person said. "He says it's an existential test of character."

I had a response to that, but before I could say it Tan Windbreaker walked by on the other side of the street.

"Hold this for second," I said, giving the pizza back to the visibly confused delivery person. I walked down the entrance stairs and into the street, toward Tan Windbreaker. My phone was in my pocket; I took it out and set the camera to record video.

Tan Windbreaker didn't notice me at first, but halfway across the street I entered his peripheral vision and he jumped slightly.

"Hey!" I said.

Tan Windbreaker started walking faster. "Hey!" I repeated, and then he broke into a run.

"Where you going?" I yelled at his back, but he was already down the street. I watched him run and turn the corner. Whoever he was, he'd just blown his cover. In fact, he'd blown his cover long before, but now he was aware of the fact. I considered the wisdom of letting him know I knew he was there. In retrospect, it probably wasn't the smartest thing I could've done. But it was too late for that now.

So, I thought, *as long as I've blown one cover, I might as well blow a couple more.*

Ten seconds later I was standing over a domestic sedan parked three spots down the street from my apartment, on the other side of the street. The two plainclothes policemen inside had watched me walk up and were visibly annoyed they'd been made by me. They watched me sourly as I tapped on the driver's side window.

The window rolled down and the cop in the driver's seat, a man with a moustache distressingly similar to Tan Windbreaker's, looked up at me. "Jesus Christ. What?"

I pointed down the street. "You saw that?"

"Saw what?" he asked.

"The guy in the tan windbreaker."

"What about it?"

"You saw him run when I called to him?"

"So what? You run up on a guy, what do you expect?" the cop said.

"He's been following me all day."

"Okay. And?"

"You know he's not a cop, right?"

"So?"

"Maybe you should follow up on that."

"Why?"

"Because he's not a cop," I repeated. "And he's been following me all day. That doesn't strike you as, I don't know, odd?"

The cop looked at his partner and then back at me. "Not our problem."

"Some dude tailing someone you really want to be a suspect in a cop death is not your problem?"

"Nope." This was drawled out laconically.

"What if he walked into my apartment and took at a shot at me? Would it be your problem then?"

The cop looked back at his partner. "We might think about calling it in then."

"Hey, I got other customers," the delivery woman said to me from the porch.

I waved acknowledgment to her and turned back to the cop. "You're bad at your job. I want you to know that."

"Man, get the fuck back into your apartment," the cop said, and rolled up his window.

"What was that about?" the delivery person asked as I retrieved my dinner.

"The Hawaiian pizza police," I said. She grinned.

As I ate my pizza, which was very good despite being made by someone who disdained the toppings, I stared at the good photo I had taken of Tan Windbreaker. As I began my second slice, I pulled up the video of Tan Windbreaker, getting a momentary but futile thrill out of watching the man jump before he broke out in a run.

The part of me who was a professional felt a little sorry for him; getting caught by the person you're tailing is never a good thing. Whoever Tan Windbreaker was, he was going to catch hell back at the office, wherever or whatever "the office" might be. The part of me who was pissed off that I was being tailed by both the cops and unnamed thugs wasn't sorry for him at all. *To hell with this guy,* I thought. *I hope his boss does break his fingers, or whatever.* But even though I'd made Tan Windbreaker, it didn't mean whoever sent him to tail me would stop. They'd just send someone I wouldn't recognize, and who might possibly be better at his job. Someone who I wouldn't see tailing me. Until it was too late.

"Who are you?" I asked Tan Windbreaker, as I ran the video one more time. He was a thug, obviously. But whose? And why?

I grabbed another slice of pizza and went to one of the windows in my apartment that looked out over the street. Three spots down, a car had pulled up to the domestic sedan the plainclothes cops were sitting in. Someone was leaning out of the car, talking to the cop on the driver's side. It didn't appear to be a particularly pleasant conversation; I suspect I was the topic.

It was obvious the cops tailing me were going to be no help in figuring out who Tan Windbreaker was. I could send the photo to Langdon, but I'd already made it clear to her I was sticking to her "we're not talking" rule. I didn't want to break that just yet. Besides, she had already seen him and told me about him. If she could've ID'd Tan Windbreaker, she would've told me.

Maybe.

Fortunately, I knew at least one other person who might have a line on who Tan Windbreaker was.

CHAPTER

NINE

A Ford Transit van rolled into the passenger pickup area of the Rosemont El Station and stopped where I was waiting. The passenger side window rolled down, and I could see Mason Schilling looking at me from the driver's seat.

"Do you have your phone on you?" he asked, over what I assumed was whatever was playing on WXRT.

"You told me not to bring it," I said. "So I didn't."

"Good. Get in," he said.

I got in. We rolled away.

"This is roomy," I said, as I buckled up.

"We're carrying toddlers," he said, tilting his head slightly to indicate the seats behind us. They were filled with ten or so twentysomethings, most of whom looked to be some degree of lit. Mason spoke loudly enough that I could hear him, but just barely. This had to be intentional, because Mason wasn't exactly the quiet sort. He wanted his voice to be muddled by the radio.

"Who are they?" I asked.

"They're our clients for the evening."

"Our clients?"

"You asked a favor of me," Mason said. "I'm asking a favor of you."

"I can already see I'm going to regret this," I said.

Mason shrugged. "Not if everything goes well."

"And if it doesn't go well?"

"Then that's what I have you for," Mason said.

"Are you going to at least tell me what we're doing?"

"We are giving our clients a one-of-a-kind thrill experience they can't get anywhere else."

"This is where I should probably tell you to let me out of the van," I said.

"Too late, we're about to get on the highway." Mason directed the van toward I-90, heading west.

"Also, since when do you own a van?"

"I don't. It's a rental."

"You rented a van?" I asked. For Mason, this was shockingly sloppy. A rental van would have GPS and other equipment that would report its every movement to Hertz or National or whatever company it had come from. Mason specialized in events whose legality was questionable at best. He wouldn't want to be tracked by a car rental place.

"Not me," Mason said, and jerked a thumb backward. "Him." I looked back to a twentysomething in the first passenger row. He was the only one of the passengers who didn't look lit. He looked miserable, in point of fact.

The miserable dude saw Mason indicating him and took that as his cue. "You're going to get this rental back in time, right?"

"No, I'm not," Mason said, and the miserable dude looked confused. *"I'm* not here. Neither is my associate. *You* are driving your friends out of town for an evening of fun, and tomorrow morning you'll find the van at a location I'll inform you about later, and then *you'll* return it."

"And it'll be in one piece?"

"That's entirely up to your pals, my dude," Mason said, indicating the rest of the passengers, who were happily whooping it up. Miserable Dude turned his attention to them, telling them to calm down. They laughed at him.

"He seems nice," I said to Mason.

"He's the dude these other assholes keep around because he's got money and the willingness to put up with their shit so he doesn't have to be alone," Mason said. "Which works out great for me."

"So where are we going?" I asked.

"Out a ways. You'll know when we get there."

"I am not thrilled with all this mystery."

"Relax," Mason said. "Anyway. It's ten now, and if everything goes well, we'll be back by two. If it doesn't go well we'll be back earlier than that."

"Can we talk about what I asked you about?"

Mason glanced back briefly. "Let's not talk in front of the children." I opened my mouth to protest. "Don't worry, my friend," he said. I noted that at no point in our conversation had he used my name, or referred to me as anything other than his associate. "I have what you're asking for. We can discuss it later." And then Mason shut up for the rest of the drive. I did, too. At one point, one of the twentysomethings offered me an edible. I politely declined.

An hour or so later, the van rolled past the hamlet of Wonder Lake, Illinois. It came to a stop a short way from the village, in a weed-filled driveway that terminated at two shacks and the base of what looked like an abandoned water tower. The base of the water tower gave every indication of being a solid argument for tetanus shots.

"Do me a favor," Mason said to me as he parked the van. "Do what I ask of you, don't look surprised, and don't talk a lot."

"This sounds *great*," I said. Mason grinned and turned off the engine, motioning at the twentysomethings to pile out of the van. He opened the center console and pulled a canvas bag and a flashlight out, and then reached in for something else and handed it to me. It was a walkie-talkie. I raised my eyebrows at this, but as requested I said nothing.

Two minutes later, all ten of the twentysomethings were out of the van and standing in front of Mason, who shone the flashlight at them. Since the van's headlights had gone out, his flashlight was the only source of light.

"Anyone else got a light?" he asked the twentysomethings. "I just realized it's dark out here." There were some laughs, and a couple of them pulled out their phones to turn on the flashlights.

"So, you just made your first mistake," Mason said, and the twentysomethings went silent. "I told you that no phones were allowed on this trip, and look, at least two of you went ahead and brought them. So here's the deal." Mason held up the canvas bag. "Your phones go into the bag, now, or we don't do this thing. All of you, turn off and give up your phones, even those of you who were too smart to fall for me asking for a light." He tossed the bag to me. "Round them up," he said. I went to each of the clients and retrieved phones. There were four total.

"Who brought a wallet or purse?" Mason asked after I collected the phones. "Don't lie because I'll know soon enough." Three hands went up. "There's your second mistake. I told you not to bring those either. Give them up to my associate. Now." I did another round, collecting two wallets and a small purse.

"We're going to get those back, right?" one of the twentysomethings asked.

"Obviously," Mason said. "Unless you piss me off any more than you already have. Now. Payment. Two hundred fifty dollars each, in cash. Right now. Get it out, count it out in front of my associate, drop it into the bag. If you don't have the money, you don't get to go on the ride. Let's see it."

Another round of collections. Nine of the ten had the cash in envelopes. The tenth sheepishly admitted to me that he'd had the money in his wallet. I retrieved his wallet from the bag and he counted out the $250, returning the money and the wallet into the bag.

"Final pregame requirement," Mason said after I'd collected the money. "Let's see your notes. All of you have to have them. All of them have to be appropriate to the moment. Show them to my associate. If he doesn't approve of the note, you don't get to go on the ride. Pull them out."

"If he doesn't approve, do we get a refund?" one asked.

"No refunds," Mason said. There was a groan at this. "I'm not running a fucking retail outlet, kiddies. Get out your notes."

I went to the first twentysomething, who had pulled out a note and offered it to me. I read it, squinting at the handwriting in the shitty glow of Mason's flashlight.

Rachel broke up with me and I spend every day at a job I hate, it read. *Honestly, what's the point. I'm getting off this planet now. Love you Mom and Dad. Sorry.*

It was a suicide note. Short, sweet, and to the point.

Suddenly, and very late in the game, I realized why we had congregated at an abandoned water tower on the very outskirts of the Chicago metropolitan area.

The nine other notes were of a similar tone, and more or less the same length, except for one, which went to seven pages in a cramped, tiny hand, single-spaced.

"Dude," I said to that twentysomething. It was the one who had rented the van.

"I know," he said. "Sorry. It got a little intense."

I nodded to Mason. They all checked out.

"Keep your notes on you," Mason said. He swung the flashlight around so that it illuminated the rickety ladder leading up to the water tower. "Now. There's a railing that goes all the way around the water tower. That ladder leads up to it. We're going up that ladder now. All of you, then me. I want to be very *very* clear that once you go up the ladder, there's only one way down. It does *not* involve the ladder. So if you're having any last-minute heebie-jeebies, this is the time to bail out. Once you get on the ladder, there's no backing out. And even if you back out, there are no refunds. So. Anyone chicken?"

No one was chicken, not even the miserable dude.

"Then up you go," Mason said. The twentysomethings filed over to the ladder and started hauling themselves up it, laughing and hollering as they did so.

"They're paying you to throw them off the water tower," I said, walking up to Mason.

"That they are," Mason said. "And they're not the first group of assholes I've done this for."

I jiggled the bag. "They're not getting their phones and wallets back, are they?"

"I'm not FedEx," Mason said. "If you want the extra cash and credit cards, be my guest."

"I'll pass. Out of curiosity, how did you find this particular water tower?"

"A friend of mine told me about it. It used to be connected to the local water system, but then the village splashed out for a new water treatment plant and this one was left to rot. They'll tear it down one day. Until then, I pay a hundred dollars to the village maintenance chief every time I use it for this." Mason held up his own walkie-talkie. "I'm taking this up with me. Guess what you're going to do."

"Oh, come *on*," I said. "You're going to make me watch them?"

"You got it," Mason said. "When they come down, you check on them. If they poof, put their clothes and effects in the bag, and I send the next one down."

"And if they don't poof?"

"Well. There's a reason they all came with suicide notes."

A little less than an hour later, Mason and I were driving back into the city, alone except for a canvas bag filled with clothes, shoes, wallets, phones, and unfulfilled suicide notes.

"What are you going to do with the bag?" I asked.

"Actually, it's what are *you* going to do with the bag," Mason said.

"Got it."

Mason was going to drop me off at a diner in Ravenswood; I could toss the bag in the diner's dumpster and then get something to eat before heading home.

The business part of the evening had gone efficiently enough. Mason had lined them up at the railing and then pushed them over, screaming and hooting as they went, each landing with a variation of a sickening crunch and thud. The only hitch had been the couple who had wanted to go at the same time, holding hands. Mason had argued with them for a minute before agreeing to send them at the same time. Then he grabbed the closest one and hauled her over the side before she or her partner could do anything about it. In the few seconds after she landed but before she vaporized, I could see her expression was one of deeply annoyed surprise.

"I don't know why you do shit like this," I said to Mason.

"A gig's a gig," he replied. I guess I couldn't argue with that. What those twentysomethings had asked Mason to do wasn't legal, but it couldn't be said that they didn't know what they were getting into. They were looking for a thrill, and a close call with death, and that's what Mason provided them—no more, no less.

"I'll be doing this again in a couple of weeks, if you want in," Mason said. "I'll need a spotter then, too. And unlike this time, I'll even pay you."

"I'll pass."

"You do you," Mason said, agreeably enough. "Although I know these days you're not as picky about your gigs as you were a couple of years ago. I know you recently took a gig I suggested you for."

I looked over to Mason sharply. "The one at Wilson Barnes," I said.

"That's the one. It's something I thought you would see as just respectable enough. Seeing that it involved a white-shoe law firm and all."

"Why'd you think of me?"

"Because we go back," Mason said. "And because when I don't have time to handle something myself for a client, the next best thing is to recommend someone good. That keeps the client happy, and keeping a client happy is the secret to return business. And because I wanted to see what you were comfortable with these days. Now I know."

I looked back to the road. "It looks like I'm comfortable with a lot of things these days."

"Nah. Tonight was you working with a situation I put you in because you needed something from me. It's not the same thing. You're still trying to keep yourself from getting too dirty. Which is fine. Silly, but fine."

"Speaking of things I need from you," I ventured.

"Ken Harrison," Mason said. "The guy in the tan windbreaker. That's Ken Harrison."

"Okay, but who *is* Ken Harrison?"

"Interesting guy, Ken. Works in the back at Gerhard's Meat Market most days, hacking down pig carcasses. Plays a fucking musical saw, of all things, in a band every Monday at Bernice's on Halsted. Has a few other side gigs of varying legality, but then, who among us these days does not. And every now and then, he picks up a gig for a small family business you have a little bit of history with."

I thought about that for a second. "Tunney," I said. The Tunneys were one of Chicago's most storied crime families from the Prohibition Era forward, although the latest generation, headed by Brennan Tunney, was allegedly trying to take the family legit. Emphasis on the word *allegedly*.

"I didn't say Tunney," Mason said. "I didn't even imply Tunney. If you inferred Tunney from the words that I have said, that's on you."

"That doesn't make sense," I said. I indeed had a history with the Tunneys, but the last time I had any interaction with them, I had done Brennan Tunney a favor, earning one currently unredeemed favor in return. The idea that the Tunneys might now be targeting me was disturbing, to say the least.

"I don't remember you asking me to make things make sense," Mason replied. "You asked me who the guy in the tan windbreaker was."

"How did *you* know who he was?" I asked.

Mason glanced sideways at me. "You're asking me how a man handy with saws, both musical and other-wise, might be useful for me to know, given my clientele and its interests and tastes?"

I opened my mouth to respond but then decided that, as a matter of fact, this was one of those times when I genuinely *didn't* want to know a single bit more than I already did. So I shut my mouth again. Mason noted this and grunted. We were silent most of the way back into Chicago.

Mason dropped me off in Ravenswood; I grabbed the canvas bag and hauled it out of the van. "What're you going to do with the van?" I asked.

"Drive a couple of miles and then leave it in a neighborhood that will terrify that whiny little shit," Mason said.

I grinned, and then stopped grinning. "What do you think Brennan Tunney wants with me?"

"I don't have the slightest idea," Mason said. "But if he's told Ken Harrison to keep tabs on you, that's not a great sign. I'd figure it out before Ken decides to play his saws on you, my friend." He pointed to the canvas bag. "Take care of that first, though." Mason put the van into gear and drove away.

I ditched the bag in a dumpster, got a coffee to go from the diner, and called a cab to take me home.

It didn't. My street was blocked with fire and police units. I paid my driver and walked the rest of the way.

There was a smoking ruin where the place I lived used to be. Behind the brick exterior, the apartment building had burned almost entirely to the ground.

"How are you?" Nona Langdon asked me.

"Homeless," I said. "How are *you?*"

I was sitting on the curb a bit down from the remains of my building, which was inaccessible due to the mass of fire trucks and police vehicles in front of it. Langdon had found me there not long after I arrived.

"The police and the fire department want a statement from you," she said. "I volunteered to get it."

"I wasn't home when it happened."

"Do you want to tell me where you were?"

"Not particularly," I said, and Langdon frowned. "Why? Am I a suspect?"

"How well did you know Angel Nichols?" Langdon said.

I frowned. Angel Nichols was my downstairs neighbor. "I said hello to her when I saw her, otherwise not at all. She mostly kept to herself. Why?"

"The investigators have some more work to do, but given the time frame and the evidence, the working theory is that sometime around midnight she decided to douse her entire apartment and the interior stairwell of your building with gasoline and then light a match. She went up and your apartment building burned down."

"She's dead?"

"Very dead."

"And the Spencers?" They were the couple on the third floor.

"Got out through the fire escape. Them and their cat. They're the ones who called it in. Them and most everyone else on the block. They said on the way down they pounded on your back door but you didn't answer. When I was notified I tried calling you but I got your voice mail. We were working on the assumption you burned up, too, until you came strolling up the street. Why didn't you answer your phone?"

I pointed in the direction of the burned-out building. "It was in there."

"You went out without your phone."

"I do that sometimes."

"If memory serves, dispatchers do that when they're doing something they're not supposed to be doing."

"I didn't have any illegal plans when I went out this evening," I assured Langdon, which was true, as far as it went. "I just left my phone at home."

Langdon frowned again but said nothing. "Do you know if Angel Nichols was in any sort of financial trouble?"

"Like I said, I didn't really know her. If she was, she didn't tell me. But even if she was, she was a renter. Burning down the building wasn't going to get her anything more than what her renter's insurance covered, if she had any."

"That was my thought, too," Langdon said.

"Are you sure it was her who did it?"

"We have her remains and a bunch of gasoline containers in the apartment. We're working with your property manager to look at the video that was uploaded to the security company's server. At this point we're ninety-nine percent sure she did it."

"So, suicide," I said.

"There are a lot less painful and messy ways to do that. Can I ask you a professional question, Tony?"

"What is it?"

"If you had been home when the building went up and hadn't been able to escape, would you have been able to come back?"

"You mean, because Angel committed arson?" I said. Langdon nodded.

"I mean, I don't make the rules here. You know that," I said.

"I know that. I'm asking for your opinion, based on your professional experience."

"I'd say it depends on her intent," I said. "If she burned down the building because she wanted me or the Spencers to die in the fire, then we'd probably come back. But if she did it with the assumption that we'd get out through the fire escape, like the Spencers did, then our deaths would be accidental. The intent wasn't there. So in that case, I'd be dead."

"That's fucked up," Langdon said. "That you'd be dead if she didn't *mean* to kill you."

"The universe's sense of irony has been on overdrive in the last several years, yes," I agreed.

"One of the reasons we thought you were in the building, aside from you not answering the phone, is that our guys didn't see you leave tonight." Langdon motioned at the car where the plainclothes cops hung out. They were leaning against it and looking sourly at me, as if it was my fault for still being alive.

"That's because, and speaking of irony, I left by the fire escape door this evening," I said.

"Why did you do that?"

"Because it's the door I was closest to when I decided to leave."

"Is that the only reason?"

"Are you asking if I also intended to sneak past your pals?" I said.

Langdon shrugged.

"It wasn't *why* I did it, no, although I was aware that it would be a side benefit. I wasn't trying to avoid them. I just *did*. Why?"

"So as far as anyone can tell, you were at home last night."

"I suppose," I said. "I didn't make a big announcement on social media that I was going out. Why?"

"Walk with me for a second," Langdon said. I looked at her doubtfully but got up. We walked to the end of the street, turned, and then walked up the alley behind the houses and apartment buildings on my street. We stopped at where my building was standing, the brick exterior smoky but still intact, fire escape still firmly attached. She pointed to the second floor, at my fire escape landing. "Tell me what you see."

I squinted. "What the hell is that?"

"You tell me," Langdon said.

"I don't know." I looked again. "A barrel?"

"It looks to me like a fifty-five gallon steel drum," Langdon said. "The Spencers said they had to reach across it to pound on your fire escape door. It was propped up against it. Blocking the door."

"I didn't put it there," I said. "And it wasn't there when I left tonight."

"So sometime tonight, after you left, someone brought a steel drum up your fire escape and dropped it off, obstructing your door," Langdon said.

"Which makes no sense."

"Unless someone thought you were in your apartment tonight and wanted to make it difficult for you to escape," Langdon said. "Not *impossible,* I'd guess. With some effort you could've moved it enough to get out of your apartment. But with a fast-moving fire event like this was, a few seconds might be the difference between getting out and losing consciousness from smoke inhalation. So let me ask you again. In your professional opinion, would a situation like that count as a murder?"

"Honestly, I have no idea," I said.

"If you *had* died, the obvious assumption from everyone would be that you'd put the steel drum there because you were an idiot who used his fire escape for storage," Langdon said. "Because you'd be dead, which means it couldn't have been a murder attempt."

"Right." I was still staring at the steel drum.

"Of course, you might not even have gotten that far," Langdon added. "The fire captain tells me your neighbors said there was an explosion. Angel Nichols's windows were blown clean out, and her ceiling, which would be your floor, collapsed almost immediately. If the Spencers hadn't gotten out right when they did, there's a good chance they wouldn't have survived. So the steel drum was more of a precaution than anything else."

"I get it," I said. "You're saying someone was trying to kill me without actually being responsible for killing me."

"I'm saying that in a very short time, three people you've been in contact with have committed suicide, and the last one did it in a way that would've killed you, too, except for luck—*your* luck, not theirs. We're way past coincidence here, Tony."

"You think there's a connection."

"I know there's a connection. You."

"Besides that one."

"You tell me," Langdon said. "There's a connection with Greg and Ted Gross because Gross was robbed and Greg was investigating it. But there's no connection with them and Angel Nichols, as far as I can see. I'm not saying it's not there. I just don't know what it is. I'm guessing you don't, either."

I shook my head.

"Then we're back to you," Langdon said. "Unless you want to find a connection that I don't know about."

"Are you asking me to consult?" This was intended to come out sarcastic but ended up just sounding bitter, and I regretted saying it the moment it came out of my mouth.

Langdon understood the intent, even if the delivery was off. "Are you going to be okay?" she asked.

"Oh, probably," I said shakily. "Once I have a place to live." I pointed to the back of a building down the street. "There's an Airbnb apartment there. On principle I dislike that it exists, because it's not great for the neighborhood. On the other hand, I'm pretty sure I can rent it until I get a new place."

"I want to keep our people on you," Langdon said.

"Right, because they did such a bang-up job tonight. Thank you, no."

"I think they'll be motivated to do better."

"They still think I'm involved in killing a cop. Somehow."

"I'll tell them to start moving away from that line of inquiry."

"And you think they'll listen to you."

"I think whoever is involved in Greg's death is involved in this. You're still under investigation, Tony. But for different reasons."

"Is that supposed to make me feel better?"

"I don't imagine it will, no."

I grunted and looked back at the smoking ruin of my apartment building.

"You want to tell me where you were tonight?" Langdon asked again.

"You're persistent," I said.

"I'm concerned and I want to help," she said. "We're friends, Tony. Or were, once. I think of you as a friend, anyway. I want to figure out what's going on as much as you do."

"I was finding out who the guy in the tan windbreaker is."

"Who is he?"

"A guy named Ken Harrison. Works for the Tunneys sometimes."

Langdon gave me a look. We had a shared history with the Tunneys, going back to the first case we'd worked together.

"Yeah, I know," I said, acknowledging the look.

"I wasn't aware you were on Tunney's radar for any reason," she said.

"That makes two of us. I've gone out of my way to stay off of it."

"You take any jobs recently that intersect with Tunney interests?"

"Not that I'm aware of," I said.

"The Tunneys have fingers in many pies," Langdon reminded me.

"That's why I said, 'Not that I'm aware of.'"

"If you don't mind, I'm going to look into this Harrison character," Langdon said.

"I don't mind," I said. "I understand he plays a mean musical saw."

"What?"

"Never mind."

Langdon looked me over. "I want you to do me a favor, Tony. I want you to take a couple of days for yourself. Get yourself situated. Get some sleep. Depressurize as much as you can. You're no good to me or yourself jangled up." She looked at the apartment building. "I don't expect much of your belongings survived that."

"I have a fire safe," I said. "It's probably buried under all of that. It has documents and a little cash in it."

"I'll get it back to you."

"Inform your boys I know exactly how much money is in there."

"It won't be a problem," Langdon said mildly. "Do you need anything before then?"

I shook my head. "I have my wallet with me and they know me at the bank. I'll be fine in the short term. Thanks."

"All right. Take a couple of days and get your head right, or at least as right as you can under the circumstances. Our people will be watching out for you while you do. We'll make our presence obvious, which will be a pain in the ass for you but should keep you safe while you get yourself out from under. Is that okay?"

"Fine," I said.

"Good," Langdon said. "And when you get your head screwed on again, there's something else I want you to do for me."

"What is it?"

Langdon pointed over to the wreckage of the apartment building. "Angel Nichols is from Chicago. Her family is here. Which means her funeral and memorial service are going to be here, too. I want you to go to them."

CHAPTER ELEVEN

St. Mary Star of the Sea Church was in West Lawn, a far west neighborhood where Angel Nichols's family had lived for at least half a century. And apparently not just her immediate family, going by the conversations leading up to the funeral service. The church was filled with aunts, uncles, and cousins of various degrees, as well as childhood friends and other community members. Angel might have left West Lawn, but West Lawn very clearly had not left her. It turned out for her and her one last visitation to the church of her youth.

I sat in the back of the church so as not to intrude on the family and those who knew Angel better than I. An usher asked who I was, and when I told him, he said he was a cousin. He was politely solicitous of my housing situation and encouraged me to greet Angel's parents later on, at the graveside service. He knew they had been concerned about the other residents of the apartment building and would want to talk. I told him I would.

It was the Cook County medical examiner's opinion that Angel Nichols did not commit suicide. Instead, she had accidentally killed herself trying to set the apartment building on fire. This was a very small mercy. Angel and her family were Catholic, and while the Catholic church was far more understanding these days about suicide than it had been historically, it was still easier not to have to negotiate that issue at all. Of course, it meant Angel's family had to live with the idea that her last living act was to intentionally burn down her building and anyone unfortunate enough to be in it. It was a lot to have to process.

Family and friends filled the front three quarters of the pews. Only one other person sat with me in the back, a tall woman who kept her head down for most of the ceremony.

The woman kept to herself at the graveside ceremony as well, not only standing apart from the mass of family and friends but watching from a considerable distance away. Given that I was currently being watched by both the Chicago Police Department and the Tunney family, I wondered if she was there for me, and if so, which of the two she was affiliated with.

Those questions would have to wait, because Angel had been laid to rest, and people were now coming up to the family to pay their respects. I wanted to be one of them.

"Oh! The upstairs neighbor!" Angel's mother, Evie, said as I introduced myself and offered my condolences. "We are so very sorry."

"It's okay," I assured her. "I'm all right and the Spencers, who lived above me, are all right, too. Please don't worry about that."

"I can't help it," she said. "I don't understand why Angel…" She trailed off, grimaced, and recomposed herself. "It means so much to us that you came. You didn't have to, and we would understand if you were angry with our Angel."

"I wouldn't have missed it," I assured her, which was true for more than one reason. "I'm not angry at Angel. I promise you."

"I imagine you've spoken to the police," Evie said. "They came to talk to us the day after. We didn't have much to tell them. I hope you might've been more helpful."

"I spoke to them. I'm not sure how helpful I was." I noticed there was a line of people behind me, so I muttered condolences again and took my leave of Angel's family.

And then I walked over to the tall woman, standing by herself a few gravesites back. She looked surprised to see me coming toward her but held her ground as I approached.

"Are you here for me?" I asked.

"Is this always how you hit on people at funerals, or are you just trying it out on me?" the woman replied after a second.

I was suddenly flustered. "I'm sorry, I wasn't trying to hit on you."

"Then what were you trying to do?"

"I...it's complicated. If I told you it would make even less sense than I'm already making," I said. "I apologize for sounding like I was hitting on you."

"Thank you," she said. "Apology accepted. And no. I'm not here for you. I'm here for Angel."

"You knew her?"

"Yes."

"But you didn't speak to the family at all."

"Now it's my turn to say 'it's complicated.'"

"Try me."

She shrugged. "I don't think there's any easy way to go to a funeral and say to the grieving parents, 'Hello, nice to meet you, I briefly dated your daughter back in college when I still thought I was a boy. Oh, and also, I think she was murdered somehow.'"

"You don't think they'd handle you being trans," I said.

"Actually, it's more that I don't think they'd handle me saying I think their daughter was murdered," she said and sighed. "Anyway, that's my version of 'it's complicated.' What do you think?"

"I think you and I should go get some coffee."

The woman looked at me dubiously.

"Still not hitting on you," I said.

"We only dated for a couple of weeks," Danielle Brewer said. We were at the Dunkin' that was literally at the corner of the St. Mary Catholic Cemetery. We sat at a small table, each of us with our coffee and doughnut. "I was interested, but after a couple of dates Angel saw I was working through issues and decided that I needed her as a friend more than I needed to date her."

"How'd you feel about that?"

"When she first said it, I was annoyed and offended. And then I was scared, because she somehow figured it out."

"That you were trans."

"No, that I wasn't *happy*. That I was unhappy down to my bones. I didn't know *why* I was unhappy—well, I had a *feeling* for why I was unhappy, but I didn't have the vocabulary for it, and I would've tried to deny it anyway." Danielle waved toward the cemetery. "We both come from conservative Catholic families. Gender dysphoria wasn't something that got talked about a lot as I was growing up. I knew I liked women so I didn't think I was gay. I didn't know what was going on with me. When I got to college, I thought dating the girls there would make me happy. Angel saw through that."

"Pretty smart for a college student."

Danielle nodded. "She was always smart about people. I mean, what was up with them, once she got to know them. She didn't figure out I was trans, which was fine because I didn't know it either. But she was the one who encouraged me to use the school's mental health service to figure out why I was unhappy." She smiled. "Only two years to figure it out."

"That's not bad."

"Well, I was unhappy for other reasons, too," Danielle said. "We had to work through all of those issues first."

"Angel never told her parents about you?"

"No, she did. They knew she had a trans friend. I don't think they knew we dated pre-transition. Angel told me that her parents would've preferred that she never dated *anyone* before marriage."

"But you never met them before today."

"Did you take all your college friends home to meet your parents?" Danielle asked.

"No, that's true," I admitted.

"I didn't stay back at the funeral because Angel had kept me a secret. I stayed back because I didn't want to say something *stupid*. Like that I thought she was murdered. I'm not great at filtering myself. You might have noticed." Danielle took a sip of her coffee.

"Why do you think she was murdered?" I asked.

Danielle looked uncomfortable. "Most people don't think you can murder someone anymore," she said. "Murder them and have them stay dead, I mean. What do you think?"

"I'm a dispatcher," I said. "I know they can still be murdered. It just takes effort. And…creativity."

"So you don't think I'm completely cuckoo pants just for thinking Angel might've been murdered."

"No," I said. "Not just for thinking it. I promise. Tell me why you think it."

Danielle leaned forward. "Angel and I hadn't been as close as we were in college—who is, right?—but we still texted all the time and called a couple of times a month. I called her a day before she…" Danielle paused, and all the grief that she'd managed not to show in the time we'd talked caught up with her. I handed her a napkin for her eyes.

"Thanks," she said a minute later, after she got control of herself again. "Sorry."

"Don't be sorry," I said. "You don't ever have to be sorry for that."

Danielle continued. "I called her the day before she died, and she was different."

"Different how?"

"Angel had always been *bubbly,*" Danielle said, and made a face. "I hate that word. It sort of implies that the person who's bubbly is also empty-headed, and Angel wasn't that. Wasn't *ever* that. But there isn't a better word for it. She was bubbly. She was almost always happy, and she had a way of making other people happy, too. She wasn't militant about it, you know? Not like, *I'm happy so fuck you, you have to be happy around me, too.* Just who she was would make you feel better. It was the big reason I wanted to date her, all that time ago."

"Got it," I said.

"I call her the day before, and she's not that way at all. She's quiet, and withdrawn, and when I ask her things she answers 'yes' or 'no' or with a grunt. I can be oblivious to other people's moods, especially when I'm on a tear about something. But eventually even I notice, and I ask her what's up. And then there's about a minute of silence on the phone, and she tells me she got a visit from some people and it gave her a lot to think about."

"A visit."

"That's what she said. And I'm trying to figure out what that even *means,* and to get more about it from her, but she's not saying much. She's back to monosyllables. Finally I ask her, 'Look, is there anything I can do for you? Anything you need?'"

"What did she say?"

"She said, 'Just don't believe what everyone's going to say when it happens.'"

"She was talking about the building fire," I said.

Danielle nodded. "Yeah. But I didn't know that at the time, and she wouldn't tell me anything else. Eventually she said she had to go. I told her I would call her in a couple of days and she said okay to that. Then we said goodbye, and that was it. The next day I looked at the Facebook page for our college class, and people were posting pictures of Angel and talking about their memories of her."

"I'm sorry."

"I fucking *hate* that I learned about her dying from Facebook." Danielle dabbed her eyes again.

"Forgive me," I said after a minute. "I want to be clear that I'm not playing devil's advocate here, I just want to understand your thinking. Why do you think this was murder?"

"Because Angel wouldn't voluntarily stand in the middle of a room filled with gasoline fumes and set herself on fire."

"It might have been accidental," I said.

"Accidentally set herself on fire in an apartment liberally doused with an accelerant," Danielle said.

"People accidentally set themselves on fire," I noted.

Danielle looked extremely unimpressed by this argument. "You don't know this about Angel, but I do: When she was in high school, she came in second place in the city—the whole city of Chicago—at a science fair for a chemistry project."

"What was the project?"

"Please," Danielle said. "Like *I* know anything about chemistry. I barely passed it in high school. I have a degree in business administration. But she liked to brag about it when people thought that 'bubbly' meant 'brainless.'"

"Right."

"So a woman who came in second place at a science fair for a chemistry project seems unlikely not to know that gasoline is *volatile.*" Danielle took a bite of her previously neglected doughnut.

"All right, but then the evidence suggests suicide, not murder," I said.

Danielle swallowed. "Yes, it does. But that's impossible."

"Because she was bubbly?"

Danielle looked annoyed. "Of course not. You can be depressed and pretend to be happy. Ask me how I know. But I *do* know. And I know Angel. Have known her, for a dozen years. She is literally the last person in the world I would conceive of entertaining thoughts of suicide, much less a suicide like *that.*"

"You said yourself you weren't as close to her as you were in college."

"We also texted daily and talked on a regular basis. You should trust my assessment."

"I don't doubt it," I said. "I'm noting the evidence."

"Don't you see," Danielle said. "Angel was *coerced*. Somehow. Into killing herself. Into setting the apartment building on fire. She said to me not to think what she knew I would think when it happened. She wanted me to know it wasn't suicide."

"You think it's related to that visit she got."

"What else could it be? She got a visit that quote unquote 'gave her a lot to think about,' and a couple of days later she burned herself and her apartment building to the ground."

"And she didn't say anything else to you about the visit."

"No. I know it was more than one person because she said 'some people.' Other than that I have nothing."

"Have the police talked to you about this at all?"

"No, why would they? I'm not family and as far as I know, no one's looking at this as a murder. They're looking at it as accidental death by arson."

"May I give your name to a detective I know?" I asked.

"They're not going to believe me," Danielle said. "For all the reasons *you* don't believe me."

"I believe you."

Danielle looked skeptical. "I don't need your sympathy."

"Trust me, it's not that," I said. "Angel's death intersects with some other things that are going on, and my detective friend could very much benefit from hearing what you have to say."

"You're serious."

"I didn't invite you to Dunkin' for the coffee," I said.

This got a smile. "All right," she said, and gave me her contact information, which I placed into my shiny new phone.

"Thank you," I said. "The detective who will contact you is named Nona Langdon. Tell her all of what you told me about your phone call."

"I will." Danielle was quiet for a moment. "Do you think I was right?"

"About Angel?"

"About not telling her parents that I think she was murdered. Somehow."

"I do," I said. I could see the tension in Danielle's shoulders, which I hadn't previously noticed, unlock when I said that. "I think you're right. There's something more going on here. But as they say, extraordinary claims require extraordinary evidence. You don't have that, and the Chicago police don't have it. Angel's family is having to sit with the idea that she burned down our apartment building. It's not fair to them to complicate what they're dealing with, based on a phone call and a feeling."

"Even if it means them thinking their daughter is an arsonist," Danielle said.

"It's not a great situation," I said. "But for now, yes."

"Thank you," Danielle said.

"For what?"

"For believing me."

"Thank me after we clear your friend," I said.

"I will," Danielle said, and then looked at me oddly.

"What?" I asked.

"Your apartment burned down," she said.

"And everything in it, yes."

"Sorry. I warned you about the lack of filters. I was just wondering if you were actually homeless now. Not that I'm offering a floor. I have two roommates and three cats. I'm just wondering if *you* are okay. Since your apartment burned down."

"Thank you," I said. "I'm fine. There's actually an Airbnb apartment on my street. I'm staying there until I get a new place. It's perfectly fine. It's decorated in modern Crate & Barrel."

"Sounds delightfully impersonal," Danielle said.

I agreed that it was, and we made small talk for a few more minutes, and then we parted, with me promising to pass her contact information to Langdon.

Which I was doing, via text, as I walked through the door of my delightfully impersonal Airbnb, only to look up and see Ken Harrison, Mister Tan Windbreaker himself, aiming a gun at me with one hand, and holding a finger to his lips with the other.

CHAPTER TWELVE

"Uh," I said.

Harrison pressed his finger to his lips with more emphasis, as if to say, *I made the shush sign, I thought it was clear, why are you not shushing?* I nodded at this very obvious body language, stayed silent, came through the door, and closed it.

Harrison dropped his finger from his lips and lowered his weapon. "Sorry," he said quietly. "I didn't know it was you."

"It's me."

"I see that now."

"Why are *you* here, Mister Harrison?"

If Harrison was surprised I knew his name he gave no sign of it, but then again I did chase him down the street a couple of days earlier. I think he assumed I knew who he was by now. "It's not me you need to worry about," he said.

"Really." I made no pretense of not eyeing his gun.

Harrison acknowledged this with a shrug. "If I was going to hurt you, I wouldn't use a gun."

I tried very hard to keep the images of saws out of my brain. "If I don't have to worry about you, who do I have to worry about?"

Harrison motioned with his head. "Come with me." He walked the short distance down the hall to the bedroom.

There were two men on the bed, one conscious, the other less so, bound and propped up. Both were bloody, which meant the bed's sheets and pillows were bloody, too. I winced at that and looked over to Harrison.

"Sorry," he said. "There were two of them. I wasn't able to be neat about it."

I squinted. "What did you tie them with?" I had come to the Airbnb with literally only the shirt on my back. Whatever he tied them with, it didn't come in with me.

Harrison reached into an interior pocket of his tan windbreaker and produced a roll of duct tape.

I stared at it blankly. "You travel with a roll of duct tape," I said.

"It comes in handy," Harrison said. "You never know when you're going to need it."

"Is this something you do all the time? Or just for... occasions like this?"

"I've done it since I was a kid. You'd be surprised at what it's useful for."

I glanced over at the duct-taped dudes on my bed. "I suppose I would be."

"I want to be clear I was not intending to duct-tape you," Harrison said. "Also, I was told to invite you to a meeting."

"You broke into my apartment to invite me to a meeting."

"I didn't break in. The owner let me in."

"You know the owner?"

"Actually, *you* know the owner. He's the one who wants to have the meeting with you."

I waved at the men on my bed. "And these two?"

"They broke in."

"Before or after you did?"

"After. They were surprised to find me."

I motioned to the bed. "Evidently. Who are they?"

"I don't know," Harrison said. "But they were breaking in, so they were up to no good."

"*You* broke in."

Harrison shook his head. "I had a code."

I decided not to argue with him about it. I looked over to the conscious one, who watched me but didn't say anything, since his mouth was duct-taped shut. "You didn't kill them," I said to Harrison.

"I don't like doing that," he said. "And anyway I was told not to. If I kill them, they just go back where they came from. My boss wants them where he can find them."

The conscious one audibly sucked air in through his nose at that.

"What's your boss going to do to them?"

"He wants to ask them questions."

"He wants to ask me questions, too," I pointed out.

"There's asking questions, and then there's *asking questions*," Harrison said. "He's particularly interested in why they came here with what's in that." He pointed to a manila folder on the bedroom dresser. Also on the dresser were two guns and what looked like the contents of the men's pockets.

I went over to the dresser and looked into the folder, and then pulled out what was in it.

They were photos. Of Nona Langdon. And of where she lived. And of her with a small child who I knew was her nephew Royce, age five.

I looked over to the conscious man on my bed. "I'd like to know why they came here with these, too," I said. I started walking over to the bed to rip the duct tape off the man's mouth, but Harrison stepped over to block me.

"I don't recommend that," he said.

"Why not?"

"They came here for you," Harrison said. "Whatever they're doing, they're doing it to get you to do something. You take that tape off, he's in control of the situation."

"He's duct-taped to a *bed.*"

"Doesn't mean he won't get in your head."

"You could threaten him for me."

Harrison shook his head. "These guys aren't amateurs. It's not gonna work on them. Plus, the fact that he and his pal are still alive means he knows I'm not supposed to kill him. Which means I can't do anything that *might* kill him, even accidentally. Especially accidentally. So there's no threat." He motioned at the guy. "Besides, it sounds like he already has some idea who I work for. You heard him suck in when I said my boss wants to keep him around. You and my boss have the same questions, I'm guessing. My boss is going to be better at getting answers."

"I could still try."

"I'd have to stop you," Harrison said. He patted his tan windbreaker, where the duct tape was.

I sighed. "So what now?"

"We wait until the cleanup crew arrives, and then you and I go to meet my boss."

"'Cleanup crew'?"

"Not *that* kind of cleanup. The other kind of cleanup."

"We need to wait for them?" I said.

Harrison motioned to the guys on the bed. "We can't leave them here unattended."

"So we let them in and we go, and they take care of this."

"We don't have to let them in," Harrison said. "They have a code."

The pub was named River Liffey and was on Armitage in Lincoln Park. It wasn't yet open. There was a small private room in the back of the pub. Brennan Tunney was sitting in it when I arrived. After I had been relieved of my new phone, I was invited to join him.

"Tony Valdez," he said, getting up from his chair and coming over to shake my hand like we were old friends. "So good to see you again. It's been, what, two years?"

"Something like that." I shook his hand and let myself be guided to a seat at Tunney's table. Tunney sat down as well, not across from me but diagonally. His men did not sit, and neither did Harrison, who had accompanied me.

The last time I'd seen Tunney, he'd asked me to do a favor for him, which I agreed to, and then he had me murdered, which I emphatically had not agreed to. I'd been avoiding entanglements with him since then, because I did not enjoy how our discussions ended.

"A long time," Tunney agreed. "Would you like a beer? Something harder? Technically the pub's not open, but I think we can do for you."

"I'm fine."

Tunney nodded to a flunky. "I'll have a pint." The flunky immediately left to acquire the beverage. Tunney turned his attention to me. "Your temporary apartment all right?"

"Yes," I said. "Well. It was, until I came back today and found your guy in it, and two other guys bleeding on the duvet."

"I do apologize for that. Harrison here is usually more discreet. But sometimes you don't get to choose the fight. The men who picked up the garbage in your apartment also came with a new set of bedding. When you go back later it'll all be cleaned up."

"Thank you."

"I'm not charging you for the duvet, either."

"I appreciate that," I said.

The flunky returned with a pint of what looked like Guinness and a small bowl of nuts. Tunney took the pint, raised it in a small salute to me, and drank. "It's almost a coincidence, you renting an apartment from me," he said as he set down his pint.

"Mister Tunney—"

"You can call me Brennan," Tunney said, interrupting me. "I think you've earned it at this point."

"—I'm not sure I see how my unintentionally renting an Airbnb from you is relevant to anything."

Tunney smiled. "I assure you it is, Tony. Indulge me for a moment." He took another sip of his pint and set it down. "The last time we spoke, you'll remember that I told you that the Tunney family's interests were now entirely legitimate."

"You did," I said, and glanced meaningfully at Harrison, who had just beaten and tied up a pair of men who had come to my living quarters for some as-yet-unnamed nefarious purpose.

Tunney caught the glance. "Point taken. Some habits are hard to break. Nevertheless, in fact, the Tunneys' businesses are now entirely above board. One of them, as you are now no doubt aware, is a business that converts apartments into temporary rentals. Noninvasively, of course. We buy the buildings, wait for the tenants to move out, and then once they're gone convert the apartments."

"I imagine you find ways to make it uncomfortable for the current tenants to stay very long once you buy the building."

"The city frowns on that sort of thing," Tunney said mildly, not exactly denying it. "I prefer to take a soft-shoe approach in any event. Carrot, not stick. You weren't being nudged out of your apartment, were you?"

"The one that just burned down?" I asked. "You own that building, too?"

"I do," Tunney said. "Did," he amended. "What a mess." He caught my look. "I had nothing to do with what happened to it, Tony. That I can promise you."

"I'm not one hundred percent convinced."

"Fair," Tunney said. "But incorrect in this case. That building was worth more to me intact than burned down. It was solid and up to code and well-maintained. And in the line of business this company of mine is in, it makes sense not to turn entire streets into itinerant housing. I bought your building to keep anyone *else* from turning it into an Airbnb and wrecking the character of the neighborhood. There's a science to this, Tony."

"If you say so."

"I do say so," Tunney said. Another sip from his pint. "The temporary rental business is immensely profitable in Chicago. The right building in the right neighborhood is a license to print money. That money comes back to us, and we send it right back out again."

"More apartment buildings in Chicago," I said.

Tunney smiled and pointed. "No. The money for the apartment buildings comes from other businesses of ours. The money *from* the apartment buildings goes to service our interests and projects in overseas markets. For example, mainland China."

"You're doing things in China?"

"It's a remarkable country," Tunney said. "A lot of people compare it to the Wild West, but I prefer to think of it as a competitive business environment."

"I've heard it referred to that way recently," I said.

"I'm not in the least bit surprised to hear that, but hold that thought. Recently, one of my companies was part of a bid in a very lucrative real estate deal over there—one that we, unfortunately, could not finance entirely on our own. Fortunately, we were able to secure a rather generous line of credit from one of the local banks here in Chicago that was looking to step up its international profile. Cermak Savings Bank. Perhaps you've heard of it."

"I have an account there."

"How interesting," Tunney said. "With that line of credit in my pocket, I got on the next plane to Beijing, because it would be advantageous for me to be there in person to make the deal. Then I arrive and discover that my primary competitor, a Mister Peng, had magically appeared in Beijing right before I got there. I believe you've met him, Tony."

I suddenly felt very cold.

Tunney apparently noticed it. "I'm not going to do anything *bad* to you, my friend." He glanced over at Harrison. "If I wanted to do that, it would already be taken care of, and there would be nothing leading back to me. The fact I'm talking to you now, in a place I know the FBI has bugged, should assure you that you're safe."

"This place is bugged?"

"The FBI bugged it. That's not the same as them being able to hear anything." He pointed to a mirror with a Guinness logo imprinted on it. "The bug's behind that. I had one of my tech guys deal with it. Now whenever I'm in here, all the FBI hears is sports talk radio. They know I've found their bug but they can't come in to fix it. It's perfect." Tunney leaned in. "It does mean they know you're here. Which is fine. I want them to know that. I want them to wonder why."

"I didn't mean to mess with your deal in China."

Tunney leaned back and waved it off. "You didn't. Well, actually, you *did*, but not intentionally. It's not your fault. I sicced the FTC and SEC on Peng to keep him busy here in the U.S. while I went to Beijing. I rushed him and that's where you came in. I should've been more careful."

"Okay, good," I said. "But you still lost the deal."

"Not then," Tunney said. "Peng's early arrival didn't work out like he planned either. He thought just showing up first with a line of credit from an American bank would help seal the deal for him. But the clients were worried about his troubles with the SEC and FTC, and were still ready to do a deal with us. Then a funny thing happened, Tony. Someone got into the servers of the Cermak Savings Bank and messed with my credit line. Not permanently, mind you. They have backups and records. Just long enough to mess with my deal and bring the clients back around to Peng. Strange, isn't it?"

"Very well timed," I said.

"Whoever did it had planned it in advance, of course," Tunney said. "But the timing of it worked well enough for Peng's purposes. His company got the deal, and mine did not. Very disappointing."

"I'm sorry."

"Thank you." Tunney dipped his head in acknowledgment. "The problem for Peng was, there were still loose ends. Because I rushed him here in the U.S., he had to go outside his usual staff and contractors to get certain things done. Those new people don't have the same loyalty to him that his other people might. And here's a funny thing about business, Tony. Loyalty works the same whether your business is legitimate or not. If you're loyal, you're an asset. But if you're not, you're a liability. And you know what happens to liabilities in business, don't you?"

"They get dealt with," I said.

Tunney nodded and sipped from his Guinness.

Suddenly I got it. I pointed at Harrison, who looked surprised to be pointed at. "He wasn't following *me* at all, was he?"

"What do you mean?"

"When I first saw him—"

"Which I'm still annoyed about. That was sloppy," Tunney said.

"—I thought he was a cop assigned to follow me. But then Detective Langdon said he wasn't of theirs.

So I thought he was some sort of thug meant to dog my footsteps."

"Technically he is a thug." Tunney looked over to Harrison. "Sorry." Harrison nodded in acknowledgment.

"But he wasn't following me at all," I continued. "He was waiting for the men who were going to threaten me to show up. Who *you* wanted for your own purposes."

"Correct," Tunney said.

"You used me as *bait*," I accused Tunney.

"I did," Tunney agreed. "And as unfortunate as your apartment burning down was for the both of us, and for poor Angel Nichols, it made catching those two men quite a bit easier. Thank you for choosing my building for your temporary housing."

"So this isn't about me at all," I said.

"No," Tunney said. "Other than that you were their target. Sorry."

"It's fine," I said, which it wasn't, but I was willing to let that go for the moment. "I was honestly confused why you cared what happened to me at all."

"Well, I still owe you a favor," Tunney said. "I feel morally obliged to make sure you stay alive until you're off my ledger."

"I...don't know how to feel about that."

"On balance, you should feel relieved."

"What happens now?" I asked.

"Now I get some questions answered," Tunney said, "and for your own sake, Tony, you should probably not ask how that's going to be managed. Likewise, if anyone asks, you and I spent this lovely time together talking about the Cubs and their pitching problems this year."

"Why did you send for me at all? You've nabbed those guys and given me a clean duvet. You didn't *need* to tell me anything else. You probably shouldn't have told me anything else at all."

"I appreciate your concern," Tunney said. "I told you as a courtesy, because as I've already noted, I have an obligation to you. I told you because it's safer for me to tell you, so you understand what's going on and don't put your nose somewhere it shouldn't be, because I know you're a curious fellow, and have a relationship with our fine police force. And I told you because now that I have these two, you're in even more danger than you were before."

"Excuse me?" I said.

"I'm going to get information out of these men, Tony, make no mistake about that," Tunney said. "While I do that, someone might notice they're gone. When that happens, whoever is holding their strings is going to come for you and anyone else they think is a danger to them. So consider this a head start. All their loose ends will be tied off as quickly as possible. You might want to lay low for the next few days. And if there's anyone else you think is in real danger because of all this, you might want to let them know, too. Sooner than later."

CHAPTER

THIRTEEN

"Are you going to tell me what this is about?" Nona Langdon said as I slid into the passenger side of her car. She was picking me up outside the River Liffey Pub. She looked inside the pub as if she was looking for someone. I think she suspected Tunney might be in there.

"Not yet," I said, and buckled in. "Did you get that address I asked you for?"

"I did," she said. "Although it took some doing. Telling me to look for a translator named 'Chen' did not exactly narrow things down, Tony."

"But you found him."

"Yes. Aaron Chen. Lives near IIT. Corner of 35th and State."

"We should go there."

"Now?"

"Yes, now."

Langdon gave me a look but put the car into drive. "And we're going there now why, exactly?"

"Because his life's in danger."

"How?"

"Suicide."

"As in, imminently."

"I think so."

Langdon reached for her police radio. I put my hand on her arm. "Don't do that," I said.

"You said the danger was imminent," Langdon said. "It could take us a half hour to get there. We have units in the area that can be there in a minute and a half."

"If a police car rolls up on him, you might make things worse," I said. "He's not a U.S. citizen. He might think they've showed up to deport him or something."

"That's not Chicago PD's job."

"You know that. Chen might not. I'd prefer to err on the side of caution."

Langdon looked skeptical, but put her hand back on the wheel.

"Thank you," I said.

"Who is this Chen person?"

"He and I did a job together recently."

Langdon glanced over at me. "What kind of job?"

"The sort of job I probably should have a lawyer present for before telling you."

Langdon looked like she was going to say something about that comment but held it in at the last second. "And this was a job that would drive him to kill himself."

"It might."

"*You* seem fine about it, though."

"It was a close thing, I think."

"All right, *that* sounds like something I need to know about."

"Let's go find Chen first," I said.

"It's going to be a little while before we get there," Langdon said. "If we're not going to talk about you or Chen, what other topic do you suggest to pass the time?"

"Let me tell you what I learned at Angel Nichols's funeral," I said. I spent the next twenty minutes catching her up on my conversation with Danielle Brewer.

Aaron Chen's apartment was on the border of the Illinois Institute of Technology. It was a unit directly above a Starbucks, a fact that would constitute a working definition of hell for me. Langdon looked up at the apartment unit as she got out of her car. "Well, I guess we don't have to worry about him jumping," she said. "You think he's home?"

"I have no idea," I said.

"Great," Langdon said, and went hunting for the entrance to the apartment units. I looked into the Starbucks, which was filled with college students, and then turned around to look up at the high-rise across the street, which went up twenty stories or so.

At the very top, on the roof, someone was peering over the corner.

"Langdon," I said, and then again, louder, when she didn't respond.

She came back to me on the sidewalk. "What?"

I pointed to the top of the high-rise. The person who had been peering over now looked like they were climbing up on the edge of the roof.

"Oh, you have *got* to be joking," Langdon said, looking up.

"I think we have to worry about him jumping after all," I said.

It was in fact Chen on the roof, and once Langdon had flashed her badge at building security, we were allowed on the roof. We walked over to the corner where Chen was now sitting, on the other side of the railing, where the lip of the roof was slightly higher than the rest of it.

Chen heard and then spotted us coming. "Don't come any closer," he said. "I'm going to jump."

"You don't have to do this," Langdon said, stopping her advance but holding out her hand. "Come on over to the other side of the railing, Mister Chen."

Chen shook his head. "I do. I do have to do this. I don't have a choice."

"Who did they tell you they'd hurt?" I asked him.

"What?" Chen looked over to me.

"Who did they tell you they'd hurt?" I repeated, and stepped a little closer to Chen. "There had to be someone. Someone you cared about. Someone you loved."

"How do you know about that?" Chen asked.

"Look at me," I said. "You remember me, right?"

It took Chen a second. "You...you're the dispatcher."

"That's right. We worked a job together. They paid us to keep quiet, remember?" Chen nodded. I took another step closer. "But it turned out it wasn't enough, was it? So they came back and told you they'd hurt someone, didn't they? I know because they tried to do the same thing to me."

"Who?" Chen asked.

I pointed at Langdon. "Her."

"What?" Langdon said behind me, under her breath. I ignored her for now.

"Why her?" Chen asked.

"Because I care about her. She cares about me. We're friends." I looked back to Langdon. "Some of the time, anyway. They knew that about me. They planned to use it as leverage against me."

"You're still alive."

"I am," I said. I held out my hand and took another step to him. "You don't have to do this, Aaron. Come back over the railing. Let us help you."

Chen shook his head again. "They're watching me. They told me if I didn't do this today, it would be too late."

"Were you visited by two men, Aaron?" I asked.

Chen opened his mouth as if to ask how I knew, but then remembered. He nodded his head. "Yes."

"Those two are out of commission for now," I said. "I know this for a fact. You have more time than you think. Tell us what they told you, and we can help protect the people you care about."

"It's not that simple," Chen said.

"I know it's not that simple," I assured him. "But I'm asking you to trust me. We can help you. Langdon here is Chicago Police. We can keep you safe. We can keep the people you care about safe. Just come back. We can do this."

Chen was quiet for a moment, then stood, turned, and looked like he was about to come over the railing. Then he reached down, grabbed the railing, and pulled himself into it, to gain momentum to push off into the air.

Langdon shouted, "No!" and reached out her hands toward Chen.

I sprinted the last few steps over to Chen as he was pushing off, and gave him a shove.

Chen's hands flew off the railing, and I caught the surprised look on his face before he tumbled down the side of the building.

I watched him fall, then turned to Langdon, her gun trained on me. "What the *fuck* did you just do, Tony?" she said, steel in her voice.

I held up my hands placatingly. "My job."

"Don't give me that bullshit."

"In my professional opinion, Chen was acting against his will when he pushed off from the railing. He was coerced into committing suicide. Just like Angel Nichols. Just like Ted Gross. Just like Greg Bradley. So I dispatched him."

"You pushed him off the building!"

"Yes, I did. And because I did, he's got a ninety-nine-point-nine percent chance of being alive in his apartment right now instead of a hundred percent chance of being dead from falling off the top of a twenty-story building. I killed him so he didn't have to die." I started to look over the edge of the building.

"Stay where you are," Langdon said. She kept her gun trained on me as she moved to the edge and then very carefully looked over. Even twenty stories up, the evidence of Chen's fall would be visible. Langdon spent a long time looking. Then she put her gun away. Apparently there was nothing to see, which meant Chen was safe for now.

"You were *sure* that pushing him would work, right?" she said. "That whoever or whatever is keeping score of these things would decide that you pushing him counted more than him jumping. Yes?"

"No," I said. "I took a chance."

"You realize that if he was dead on the street, it wouldn't matter if it was because of his suicide. I'd still have arrested you for murder. Your *job* wouldn't have covered for this."

I nodded. "I know. I decided it was worth the risk." I finally looked over the edge, straight down twenty stories. A small crowd had gathered where Chen must have fallen, streaming out from the Starbucks and the building lobby. They were looking up at the roof where he had jumped from. But there was no body, no blood, and no collateral damage. Chen had disappeared, leaving his clothes behind. So he was alive, and probably at home, naked, wondering what the hell happened.

"We need to get to him before he thinks to give it another shot," I said. I started toward the roof door, but Langdon stopped me. "What?" I said.

"When you were talking to Chen you said people had threatened me in order to get you to try to commit suicide."

"Yes," I said, then winced. "I mean, I think they were intending to. They were interrupted before they could."

"'Interrupted.'"

"It's complicated," I said. "I'd rather not get into it at the moment. What I can say is that they brought along pictures of you. And of where you live." I didn't mention the picture of Langdon's nephew. I decided she didn't need to know that.

"So what?" Langdon said. "They were going to kill me or something? You of all people should know that doesn't usually work anymore."

"I don't think killing was what they intended to do," I said. I let that hang there for a bit.

Langdon got it. "I'm sorry, Tony," she said.

I blinked. "What are *you* sorry for?"

"For being someone they—whoever *they* are— thought they could use as leverage against you."

"Come on," I said. "It means you're my friend. I'm going to be really offended if you apologize for that."

Langdon smiled. "All right."

"It didn't work, anyway. Not yet, at least." I motioned to the roof door. "Now let's go find Chen. I think we have a lot to talk to him about."

"No, wait a second," Langdon said, and pulled out her phone.

"What are you doing?" I asked.

"People wanted Chen to commit suicide," Langdon said. "I think we better give them what they want."

"You're dead," **Langdon** told Chen in his apartment a few minutes later.

Chen looked confused. "But I'm...*not.*" He had seemed numb when he buzzed us in, and it was clear he still hadn't come entirely to grips with what had just happened. He was in a bathrobe but otherwise hadn't managed to dress himself. I gave him the clothes he jumped in. He took them blankly and set them on the kitchen table, where we were now talking.

"Yes, you are," Langdon said. "After Tony...*dispatched* you, I called in to my captain and explained what I needed from him. You've been reported as dead. A suicide in your apartment. If the people threatening you need confirmation that you're gone, they'll have it. You and your people are safe from them."

Chen processed what Langdon was saying, nodded, and then after a few seconds broke down crying. We gave him a couple of minutes to work himself out of his state.

"There are conditions," Langdon continued, after Chen had pulled himself together a bit.

"What are the conditions?" Chen asked.

"You tell us everything you know. About what happened to you. About who is doing it. And why."

Chen looked over to me. "*He* already knows. They sent people for him, too."

"Tony knows some things," Langdon said, before I could say anything. "But what he knows might not be what you know. So I want to know what *you* know. Your story, Aaron."

"You said the Chicago police would turn me in to Immigration," Chen said to me.

It took me a minute to remember when I had said that to him. "That was if my dispatching of Mister Peng had gone wrong," I said. "This is a totally different situation. No one's going to bring Immigration into this."

Chen smiled ruefully. "Your dispatching of Peng *did* go wrong," he said. "He survived." He turned to Langdon. "Peng is a very bad man, just so you know."

Langdon nodded and pulled out her notebook. "And Peng is who, exactly?"

Chen seemed surprised at this and pointed at me. "Hasn't he told you anything?"

"Tony has been selective in what he's told me so far," Langdon said.

"You didn't want to get in trouble with the police either," Chen said to me. I shrugged. Chen didn't seem happy about this.

"Aaron, who is Peng?" Langdon asked.

"He's a businessman from mainland China," Chen said, glaring at me but then turning his attention back to Langdon. "Mostly real estate from what I know, but some side businesses as well. Some not-entirely-legal side businesses, I'm guessing."

"You're guessing," Langdon said.

"I was his translator when he was talking to English-speaking people. There were meetings I wasn't allowed at where he was speaking Mandarin. He speaks the Beijing dialect of that, and I heard him speak a little Cantonese as well. Poorly."

"When you were translating for him, what was he talking about?" Langdon asked.

"Mostly about the real estate deal he was trying to get financing for here in the U.S.," Chen said. "It was the usual real estate and finance talk, but now and again he'd let slip the fact that he was in competition with a company here in Chicago, owned by someone named Tunney."

"Did he, now?" Langdon said, glancing at me.

"Yes. And that's where the talk would kind of go off the rails, legally speaking. Peng would talk about all the things he was doing here and in China to keep this Tunney person from getting the deal over him."

"And you remember what those were?" Langdon said.

"Ma'am, my job is to say things exactly. I remember exactly what was said."

"You're not Peng's usual translator, though, are you?" I asked.

Chen shook his head. "Peng's usual translator couldn't make it. Visa troubles of some sort, I was told. His lawyer recommended me. Mister Barnes. He knew me because I did translating at a law conference he attended a few weeks earlier."

"A last-minute substitute," Langdon said.

"Right. I was told that what I was hearing and translating was confidential and proprietary information. Barnes made me sign an NDA. The money was good, so I did it."

"And then what happened?"

"Then nothing happened for a while. Then two days ago I was visited by two men. They said they represented Peng on a business matter. They showed up with photos of my fiancée."

"Who is your fiancée?"

"Her name is Jeanee Han. She's an American, but she's over in Beijing right now, doing work on her doctorate. They had pictures of her, of her apartment in Beijing, of her in all the places that she usually went. They told me they knew where she was every minute of the day. And they told me that if I didn't kill myself by today, they would kidnap her and…" Chen stopped and sucked in his breath.

"I know this is hard," Langdon said.

Chen waved her off. "They didn't tell me what they would do to her. Not directly. What they did was, they told me some of their favorite techniques. To keep people alive, but in misery. The ways they liked to torture people. How they could do it for weeks or even months until someone's mind was gone, and the only thing they could do was scream and feel pain, for however long they lived after that. How this was the way things were done, now that you can't murder people anymore. And then when they were done with that, they asked me which of the techniques they just described to me I would like them to use on Jeanee."

"Or you could kill yourself, and they'd leave Jeanee alone," I said.

"Yeah," Chen said and looked at me. "They couldn't just kill me. They needed me to kill myself. But if they make me kill myself, isn't that murder? I don't want to die. Didn't want to die. How is that not a murder? You're a dispatcher. You tell me."

"I don't know," I said. "I don't make the rules, Aaron. It feels like murder to me. Murder by other means."

"So why does it work?" Chen said.

"If I had to guess, it's because you still have to agree to it. People agree to bad deals all the time."

"It's not right."

"No," I agreed. "Nothing about this is right."

Chen turned back to Langdon. "What do I do now?"

Langdon closed her notebook. "You're dead for now. We'll get a secure EMT unit over here to wheel you out in a body bag just in case anyone's watching, and then we'll get you someplace secure and safe. You're going to talk to us and probably a couple of federal agencies about everything you know about Peng."

"And what about Jeanee?"

"I have a friend in the State Department who owes me a couple of favors," Langdon said. "We'll get her into custody as quickly and quietly as we can."

"Thank you."

"You'll need to tell us everything, Aaron. No gaps."

"Ma'am, they made me jump," Chen said. "I *did* jump." He pointed at me. "Only his shove kept it from being a suicide. So they got what they wanted from me. I don't owe them anything. And I want to make them pay."

Langdon nodded. "Stay there. Don't get up. Don't answer your phone." She motioned to me and we went out of the kitchen area into the hallway.

"You think this is what happened to everyone else, too," she said to me quietly. "These guys came around to them and threatened long-term torture to people they cared about unless they threw themselves off a building."

"Or shot themselves, or walked in front of a train, yes," I said.

"And Angel Nichols?"

"They tried to get creative in taking me out. Burn down the building and have my death, and the deaths of the Spencers, look like accidental casualties."

"So not counting the Spencers, we have three quote-unquote 'suicides' and two more attempts with you and Chen here."

"More than that, I'd bet."

Langdon looked at me oddly.

"When you get back to the office," I said, "look through recent reported suicides. Look for three men, probably in their thirties, possibly dispatchers."

Langdon thought about it. "That bank robbery you were at."

"Yeah."

"You think it's connected."

"I'm pretty sure about it."

"This is news to me," Langdon said pointedly.

"Events have been happening quickly."

"Chen's not the only person who needs to start talking, Tony."

Before I answered this, my phone buzzed in the way it does when I have incoming email. I pulled it out of my pocket to see I had two new messages. I held up a finger to Langdon to put her on pause. She was not thrilled about this.

The first message was from an email address I didn't recognize. "A gift from a friend," the header read. I opened it up to read it.

A partial transcript from your visitors earlier today, it said. *Not admissible in court but very interesting. Feel free to share with your law enforcement acquaintances. More to come.* This was followed by a long block of text; it looked like someone had set a phone app to transcribe and then made someone—or more than one someone—talk.

"What is it?" Langdon said.

"Hold on," I replied.

"Tony, you're killing me over here."

I nodded and opened up the second message. It was from Lloyd Barnes, senior partner of Wilson Barnes Jimenez and Park.

Have a rush job for you, it read. *Very very lucrative if done right. How soon can you be here?*

I looked over to Langdon.

"What is it?" she asked again.

"Remember what I just said about events happening quickly?"

"Yes?"

"I think they just went into overdrive."

FOURTEEN

"You're here later than I would've liked," Lloyd Barnes said as I entered his office. He got up from his desk and shook my hand, and then looked past me to his executive assistant. "You can go now, Marjorie," he said. "Thank you for staying." The executive assistant nodded and left.

I looked around. "Where's the client?"

"They'll be here presently," Barnes said, heading back around his desk.

"You've let your assistant go," I said.

"It'll be fine. Sit, Tony." He motioned to the chair in front of the desk. I sat.

"Sorry I wasn't able to get here sooner," I told Barnes. "I was busy with another client."

"It's fine," Barnes said. "And now that I'm thinking about it, it's probably better this way. We can take care of things more quickly now."

"All right."

"Tell me, Tony—I'm going to call you Tony this time, if that's all right."

"It's fine."

"Good. Tony, did you like working for me previously?"

"I liked the money," I admitted.

Barnes chuckled. "I suppose that's fair. I know it's not a great time to be a dispatcher these days, with legitimate work harder to come by."

"It's like any job," I said. "There are ups and there are downs."

"Recently it's been mostly downs, though, hasn't it?"

"Some years are harder than others, yes."

"Is that why you participated in a robbery of the Cermak Savings Bank a couple of weeks ago?"

I blinked. "Excuse me?"

Barnes smiled, opened a drawer in his desk, and pulled out a manila folder. He placed it on his desk and slid it over to me. "Read that," he said.

I took the folder and opened it. There was a note inside from a Levi Carroll. It admitted to planning the robbery of the Cermak Savings Bank and recruiting four others to participate. The names included Doyle Hill, the robber who died on the floor of the bank, and me.

I looked over to Barnes. "What's this?"

"It's a suicide note," he said. "Levi is a client of ours—*was* a client of ours, I should say—and after the robbery attempt, when Doyle Hill was left behind as evidence, he knew it was only a matter of time before he was found out. I convinced him to write out the details of the robbery, so that when the police came to him, we might be able to get a lighter sentence in exchange for information."

"You told him to write a suicide note?" I said.

"Of course not," Barnes said. "But I think as he went along describing the events, he decided that was the better course of action. I would disagree, but I wasn't there when he decided that. I wish I had been." He pointed at the note in my hand. "Levi says that your role in the robbery was to be the lookout. You went in, made sure the place was safe to rob, and gave the signal. You were already a customer there, so your presence didn't raise any alarms, so to speak."

"It's not true."

"Of course it's not." Barnes's voice was calm and reassuring. "And even if it were, under the law, you have the presumption of innocence. But here's the thing." Barnes reached into his desk again and pulled out two more folders. "Freddie Marsh and Dominic Gibson also named you as a participant."

"Who are they?" I asked.

"That's the correct response," Barnes said. "They're the other two living participants in the robbery. Or were," he corrected himself. "After Levi committed suicide, Marsh and Gibson followed in quick order. It seems he set the tone for the crew. You excepted, Tony."

I took the folder with Carroll's note on it and tossed it back on the desk, where it settled over Marsh's and Gibson's notes. "This is a setup."

"It could be," Barnes agreed. "And in a court of law you'll have a chance to argue that. But you have to admit, Tony, that the circumstantial evidence doesn't look great. You aren't working above-the-board jobs these days. Three of the four other people involved name you as a participant. And the fourth, Doyle Hill, was someone who you knew and who texted you about a job a couple of days before he died. Maybe this particular job. Then Greg Bradley, the cop who is investigating the robbery and you, suddenly turns up dead. And then there's this." Barnes tapped the folder that corresponded to Gibson. "Gibson's note says that you came to him and threatened his children if he revealed that you were in on the job. He says that he thought his death was the only way his children would be safe from you."

"I don't even know Gibson! I've never met him in my life!"

"I believe you," Barnes said soothingly. "But it's not me you'll have to convince. It's a jury. And the charges that would be laid on you are pretty significant. Robbery. Assault. Conspiracy to murder, both for Ted Gross, the branch manager, and for each of the other participants in the robbery. Making criminal threats. And so on. It's a lot. You'll be keeping your lawyer busy."

I laughed bitterly. "Are you offering to represent me, Mister Barnes?"

Barnes spread his hands open. "Sadly, I cannot. I think the court would suggest my relationship with Levi Carroll in this matter would represent a conflict of interest. But if you like, I can recommend a number of very good defense lawyers here in the city."

"Thanks," I said.

"You're welcome," Barnes said. "But let me suggest to you another option." He reached into his desk a final time, to retrieve a Smith & Wesson M&P handgun, basic police issue.

I looked at the gun carefully. "This is the gun I used on Peng," I said.

"It is," Barnes agreed.

"And you didn't get rid of it?"

"Let's just say I thought I might have a reason to keep tabs on it. And the reason is this: It's not my gun, since I would never keep an unregistered, unlicensed, and untraceable handgun in my office. It's yours. You brought it here to our meeting, which I did, as a matter of record, invite you to, to discuss a potential job. You demanded more for the job than I was willing to pay, because you needed a significant sum to disappear after three of your co-conspirators in the Cermak

Savings robbery outed you. When I refused to pay you what you asked, you pulled the gun and attempted to rob me, as you know I keep petty cash in my wall safe. When I likewise refused to open the safe for you, you first threatened my family members, just as you'd done with Gibson, then you became despondent. And then…" Barnes trailed off and looked over at the gun.

"And then I made a mess in your office," I said.

"Well." Barnes smiled. "I do have a private bathroom."

I took the gun. "What if I just shot you with it instead?"

"There's one round," Barnes said. "You could waste it on me. If you kill me, I go home and you lend credence to my story. If you wound me, I bleed and you lend credence to my story. If you leave here without shooting anyone, you're arrested for all the charges I've already communicated to you, and I still tell my story. Which now has further credence because your prints are all over that gun, so thank you for that."

"Or I could shoot myself."

"Certainly if you did, I'd understand why. You're trapped by your own alleged actions, with nowhere to go. You don't even have a home anymore. The evidence against you, while circumstantial, is significant. If I were your lawyer, which I'm not and cannot be, what I'd suggest is that you try for a plea deal. But even with a plea deal, I can't see you getting less than thirty years before parole is on the table. Without a plea deal, you'll most likely die in prison. You don't strike me as the maximum security sort, Tony."

I broke down at this point. Still clutching the handgun, I brought my hands to my face, and then leaned forward, sobbing. From behind his desk, Barnes watched as my head bobbed up and down in time to my sobs.

After a moment, I finally came back up for air and looked at Barnes. "You weren't ever going to offer me a job, were you?"

"There *is* a job," Barnes said. "I have a client who likes jumping out of planes without a parachute. He needs someone to tandem jump with him, and at some point in the fall intentionally cut him loose. I'm going to give it to your friend Mason, I think. It's more of his kind of thing."

"And Mason knows nothing about any of this," I said.

"No. He thought he was doing us both a favor when he recommended you to me."

I placed the gun back on the desk, on top of the suicide notes. Barnes arched his eyebrows. "Not a gun enthusiast?" he said.

"They're messy."

"But quick and painless. And I would note, Tony, that it's not going to be long before the police come looking for you."

"Oh, I know they'll come for me," I said. "But probably not for the reason you think."

Barnes smiled. "And why is that?"

It was my turn to smile. "Hold that thought, councilor. Let me come at it from a different angle. Beijing is fourteen hours ahead of us. Or fifteen, one of the two, I can't remember. The point is, right now it's morning in China, and right now Mister Peng, your client, is being arrested by the Chinese authorities on a number of different charges, including bribery, conspiracy, robbery, and attempted murder."

Barnes stopped smiling. I took this as a sign to continue. "It turns out he'd cut some ethical corners on a deal he was doing, one he sought financing for here in the U.S. In doing so, he not only ran afoul of both U.S. and Chinese law—which is why he's currently being arrested in Beijing—he also ran afoul of his competitors for the deal, who include the Tunney family here in the U.S."

"I don't know anything about this," Barnes said.

It was also my turn to chuckle. "We both know *that's* not true, Mister Barnes. You know it's not true because you're you. *I* know it's not true because for the last few hours, Aaron Chen, the translator you hired to work for Mister Peng, has been busily telling the Chicago PD, the Attorney General's office, the FBI, and some other federal types everything that he heard or translated while he was working for Mister Peng—or more accurately, for *you,* since you hired and paid him directly and made him sign that NDA. Turns out NDAs aren't applicable when there's criminal activity involved. And it also turns out Chen isn't nearly as dead as he was reported to be."

Barnes stood up.

"Sit down, the cops are already here," I said. "They're downstairs, Barnes. Your executive assistant didn't make it out of the building. Right now, I'm sure she's looking at all the local, state, and federal warrants those folks are about to serve you. My job here was to keep you busy while they showed up. When they're assembled, they'll be coming up. All of them. All at once. In the meantime, I'm sure you can see them if you look out your window. Look for the flashing lights."

Barnes started to turn his head, but stopped.

I leaned in. "There's more than that," I said. "Just between you and me? There's a certain competitor of Mister Peng. I'm sure you know him. He's the one whose money you messed with by having your folks break into the Cermak Savings computer systems during that fake robbery. Well, he has his hands on the two ball-breakers you and Peng hired to threaten people's friends and families to make them commit suicide."

Barnes's eyes widened.

"Those two visited Chen, so the cops know about them. But they also visited me, which is how the competitor knew about them." I was choosing not to use Tunney's name because I liked watching Barnes's brain say it for me. "Now the competitor knows how they intimidated Greg Bradley, a cop, into killing himself, but not before he was made to leave notes to look like I was involved. The competitor knows how Angel Nichols was made to splash gasoline all over her building—a building that the competitor owned, by the way—and light it up with her in it. Peng's competitor knows all of that, and a lot more. So even if you somehow manage to skate by every single legal charge against you and your law firm, Barnes, that competitor is out there. And he wants me to let you know he's waiting for you."

"For me," Barnes said.

"Yes," I said. "And just you. No threatening your family, or friends, or law partners. Just you. And this competitor has all the time in the world for you." I leaned back.

Barnes just stared.

"Also, that bullshit about me being in on the robbery isn't going to fly," I said. "Obviously. But I give you credit for that. A nice improvisation when you didn't hear back from your guys about me today. I bet the signatures on those suicide notes might even match your victims' real signatures. And yes, we know your boys visited them, too. *All* of them. You have a lot to answer for, Mister Barnes. What do you think about that? Because I have to tell you, you don't look like the maximum security sort to me."

Barnes kept staring at me, then reached for the Smith & Wesson, held it to his temple, and pulled the trigger.

The gun made a dry *click* as the hammer mechanism hit on air.

I showed Barnes the bullet I'd cleared from the chamber when I was bent over, out of his direct line of sight, weeping and wailing.

"You're not getting out of this that easy," I said.

The doors to the law firm burst open and all manner of law enforcement streamed in, waving warrants.

FIFTEEN

"So the bank robbery was never a bank robbery at all," Langdon said as we drove toward West Lawn.

"No," I said. "It was a system infiltration to knock Tunney's line of credit offline. Barnes hired Doyle Hill, who staffed out the robbery, except for Levi Carroll. Barnes got Carroll acquitted on a hacking charge a couple of years ago and had him come to handle the infiltration on Gross's computer. Everyone would be so busy looking at the bank robbery that no one would connect it to Tunney's money disappearing. Occam's razor. The simplest explanation is the right one. Except in this case it wasn't."

"I told you I had a hunch about that robbery."

"You did," I agreed. "I'm not sure you thought it was about real estate money going *poof.*"

"But that was just an illusion," Langdon said. "The money was still there. Tunney knew it. The bank knew. Everyone knew it. They just had to find it in the system."

"Yes, and it didn't matter. The deal that Peng and Tunney were competing on was as close to 'cash on the barrelhead' as things get these days. Tunney had to show up in China with the money literally in hand, ready to transfer. The delay cost him the deal. That's China for you these days."

Langdon shrugged. "Sounds like the Wild West out there."

I smiled. "I think the euphemism they prefer is 'a competitive business environment.'"

"All I know is that it makes Chicago look tame, and that's a hell of a thing." Langdon glanced over to me. "You still haven't told me everything you know about Tunney's part in all of this."

"I don't know what you mean."

"Come on, Tony," Langdon said. "I collected you the other day outside one of Tunney's favorite pubs. You knew how the so-called robbery connected to Tunney's money before Barnes told us. You knew about the men Barnes hired to threaten everyone connected to this Peng business. And I'm betting good money you knew where they were before those two turned themselves in."

Langdon was talking about Cole Poulin and Jerr Dupre, the two medium-level bad men who'd turned up on the Chicago PD's doorstep the morning after Barnes had been arrested, eager to talk about their part in the proceedings. They confessed their roles in dazed and haunted tones but were in perfect physical shape, which suggested to me that they had been treated to a number of the techniques they had described to Aaron Chen, and then killed with the admonition to confess their crimes and otherwise shut the hell up.

Which they did, admirably. Their stories corroborated what Barnes and Chen had said, and closed the book on what happened to Greg Bradley, Angel Nichols, Ted Gross, and the robbery participants who had initially escaped. They even explained the missing pages in Bradley's notebook. The pages contained names and details of other people Bradley had been investigating, and the two of them wanted the other cops to focus on me.

The Illinois Attorney General's office would be pursuing murder charges against Poulin, Dupre, and Barnes for all of those deaths, but not for attempted murder against me, because as far as the police knew, they had never come to visit me.

Well, actually, one member of the police knew. But she wasn't telling. So far.

"I think it's best to go with what we have," I said to Langdon.

"You know that Tunney is trouble," she said. "Trouble you don't want."

"We don't disagree," I said. "I don't want his trouble. But sometimes I have to deal with it anyway."

Langdon nodded. She understood that, at least. "Maybe we can change that."

"What do you mean?"

"I mean that you helped to solve a robbery and several murders, and you were an integral part in bringing down one of the most prominent crooked lawyers in the city," Langdon said. "You're good at this. And also, when you're not working with us, you get yourself in trouble."

I smiled. Both of these things were true. "So what are you saying?"

"I'm saying that I think it's time to bring you back inside."

"You mean, to consult for the Chicago PD again," I said.

"For now. But it might be time for us to start thinking about a longer-term solution."

"Like what?"

"Like you joining us, Tony."

"What, as an actual cop?" I was incredulous.

"It's not *that* bad of an idea."

"There's no such thing as a dispatcher cop."

"There hasn't been, no," Langdon agreed. "But that doesn't mean there couldn't be one."

"A week ago the Chicago Police Department was pretty sure I was a cop killer," I reminded her. "It's a *lot* to go from that to a member of the force."

"That's why I said you'd consult for now," Langdon said. "After that, we'll see."

"You're still on an austerity budget," I said.

"I think I can make an argument about this being a justifiable expense."

"I'll think about it," I said.

Langdon looked at me. "You'll *think* about it."

"That's what I said."

"Because you have so much else going on with your career right now," Langdon said.

"I don't want to jump in on things too quickly. Also, I don't know that you can afford me."

Langdon snorted. We turned onto Pulaski and drove south.

A few miles later we parked on South Kildare, in front of one of the modest brick homes there.

"This is it," I said, staring out the car window at the house. "Angel's parents."

"That's the one thing I still don't understand," Langdon said. "Why her? Of everyone involved, she was innocent. Greg, at least, was a cop. But Angel...she didn't *do* anything but live where you lived."

"That's why they worked on her," I said. "You put cops on me. Poulin and Dupre couldn't get to me. But you didn't have anyone watching her. That's *why* they picked her. That's why they made her burn down the building. But once they realized I'd survived, they still couldn't come after me directly. They had to wait until I asked you to have your people stop following me, and I was in the temporary apartment."

"So Angel's death is my fault," Langdon said.

I shook my head. "No. It's Barnes's and Peng's. You were keeping an eye out for me. I appreciate it. You just didn't know there would be consequences for it. Neither did I." I got out of the car.

Someone was waiting on the sidewalk for us. Someone I'd asked to meet us there.

"Danielle," I said, shaking her hand, and then turning to introduce Langdon. "This is Detective Nona Langdon, who I talked to you about."

They shook hands. "Tony said I should talk to you," Danielle said to Langdon. "But I don't know why he thinks I should talk to you...here." She motioned to the house. "This is Angel's house. Her parents' house, I mean."

"Actually, we wanted to talk to all three of you," Langdon said. "About what happened to Angel. About what we know happened."

Danielle looked at Langdon, and then back at me, confused.

"You were right, Danielle," I said. "You were right. And what Angel told you was right, too. You don't have to believe what they said about her. We know the truth."

Danielle looked at both of us again, and burst into tears. I gave her a hug, and a few minutes later, when she had collected herself, we all went to tell Angel's parents the truth as well.